Just a Taste

Tiny Snapshots of Queer Love

Yolande Kleinn

Published by Yolande Kleinn, 2025

www.yolandekleinn.com

Just a Taste: Tiny Snapshots of Queer Love

By Yolande Kleinn

Book Design: Yolande Kleinn
Cover Photo: Alexander Grey
    pexels.com/@mccutcheon/
Cover Font: Millania fromthehungryjpeg.com
Cover Font: Canter from thehungryjpeg.com
Interior Font: Born from thehungryjpeg.com

First Edition April 2025

Print ISBN 978-1-946316-58-5
Digital ISBN 978-1-946316-57-8

Table of Contents

Nearly Home

Sofia wakes slowly, her body lethargic and her mind groggy with the vestiges of a pleasant dream.

Her limbs ache with the sense of having rested somewhere not especially comfortable, but Sofia doesn't mind. She often falls asleep in less-than-ideal places.

It's the curse of an irregular sleep schedule—the strange hours she keeps, balancing grad school with a part-time job—the tendency towards night owl behaviors despite a constitution more inclined to daylight.

In any case, despite her body's quiet protest and the way she's coming to realize she has folded herself up in sleep, Sofia has no desire to wake more fully. She feels safe and content. Her cheek rests on something warm, and there's something else... Some additional sensation...

Ah. The soft slide of fingers through the wild strands of her hair. The touch brushes across her scalp, again and again, nearly sending her right back into dreams.

Sofia is far too sleepy to guess who might be touching her so tenderly. Not her girlfriend—now ex-girlfriend, she reminds herself harshly. And sure as hell not the one person she wishes would touch her this way. Elena Mendez is her best friend, and if she has ever looked at Sofia with anything like tenderness, she's concealed it well. That leaves Sofia's other friends, but even this she finds almost impossible to account for. Plenty of them are physically affectionate, but this isn't the sort of contact they favor.

It's far too sweet. And Sofia's brow furrows, as the mystery drags her more alert despite her best efforts to drift away.

"Welcome back," rumbles a familiar voice, gruff with wry affection. "You've been asleep for over an hour."

Sofia inhales sharply and opens her eyes. Denim and belt loops fill her field of vision, so close they go a little blurry. She turns her head, raising her gaze to confirm—not believing even once she does—that she's been sleeping with her head on Elena's thigh.

Oh, shit. Those *are* Elena's fingers tracing idle patterns in her hair.

The cab of Elena's truck is dark but for the glow of the dashboard and a glimmer of streetlight from far overhead. There's barely enough light to see Elena's broad frame, her tousled hair, the narrow glasses on her round face. Her wide jaw with a faint, familiar scar. The flicker of a smile at one corner of her mouth.

"Where…?" Sofia tapers off almost as soon as she starts to ask, unwilling to sit up and look out the window if it means Elena will stop petting her hair.

"Rest area," Elena murmurs without taking her eyes off Sofia. "You didn't wake when I pulled off the highway *or* when I unbuckled your seatbelt. Nearly gave me a heart attack when you curled up in my lap instead. You've been completely dead to the world."

"Sorry," Sofia says. But she's not. She's pleased, and not sorry at all, and she still can't entirely believe Elena is touching her this way.

"We're nearly home."

Elena's home. Not Sofia's. When one's relationship implodes right before Valentine's Day, sometimes the only option is to call for rescue from a friend who lives two states away. She knew Elena would come collect her, short notice be damned. What she will do once the dust settles, Sofia still isn't sure, but at least she can figure it out from the reassuring comfort of Elena's couch.

"What time is it?" Sofia asks.

"Almost midnight." Elena's smile quirks higher. "Those construction zones really ate into our driving time. We'll have to refuel as soon as we hit town."

"Mmm." Sofia closes her eyes, giving a thoughtless little stretch that rubs her cheek against Elena's leg and interrupts the steady caress. Immediately Sofia wishes she'd kept still.

She blinks her eyes open again and peers up into Elena's face. Searching. Hoping. Pleading without words, and wondering how well Elena can read her in the shadows.

Elena's expression is a cryptic mystery. But after an agonizingly slow span of seconds, she licks her lips. Such a small gesture, but it makes Sofia's heart race. A moment later, Elena's touch disappears from her hair—a loss Sofia doesn't have time to mourn before gentle fingertips are trailing over her jaw, her temple, the line of her cheek.

The touch hesitates. An eloquent pause. And then the pad of Elena's thumb traces Sofia's lower lip.

"We should..." Elena starts to say, but her voice has gone raspy and she trails off. She swallows hard, seems to deliberately relax her tight shoulders. "We should get back on the road."

Even brighter hope soars in Sofia's chest at this sequence of wordless signals. She wonders if it's fucked up to be this excited about the way Elena is looking at her, in the wake of Sofia's newly imploded long-term relationship. But even her ex knows she's got it bad for Elena. It isn't the reason they broke up—not by a long shot—but it certainly didn't help keep them together.

Suddenly her hopeless crush doesn't feel so hopeless, and Sofia holds Elena's gaze as she finally pushes herself upright on the creaky leather bench seat. She catches Elena's retreating hand and holds it, achingly aware of her own racing pulse. Finally, she draws Elena's hand toward her, pressing a kiss to the warm palm.

Elena drags in a harsh breath, but Sofia just lets go in order to buckle back into her seat. "Let's finish driving. I think we're both ready to be home."

For several seconds, Elena stares at her, looking so winded and incredulous that Sofia nearly doubts her impulsive gesture.

But then Elena faces forward and turns the key in the ignition, roaring the truck to noisy life and gripping the wheel a little too tightly. Her voice is rough as sandpaper when she says, "Yes. Okay. Home." Then, sparing only a quick glance toward Sofia, she backs out of the parking stall and aims the truck for the highway.

Compromise

They've been living together for almost a year, and sometimes Tyler can't wrap his head around this fact.

It was supposed to be a temporary arrangement. A few months of him contributing rent, so Patrick could get a handle on a heavy mortgage and Tyler could have a low-stress place to live. The ideal setup, while Tyler looked for something closer to the law office where he's hoping to make partner.

But somehow, the commute hasn't bothered him like it should. How can he begrudge a little extra driving time when it's Patrick he's coming home to—big, sturdy, quiet, lovely Patrick. And for some reason, Patrick seems to like having him around. At least, Tyler assumes Patrick likes having him around. He's hard-pressed to come up with any other reason the man asked him to stay on indefinitely.

There's no way Patrick made the offer for any of the reasons Tyler's hopeful imagination might conjure. Patrick can't possibly reciprocate the bright, ridiculous feeling Tyler gets whenever he looks at his roommate and catches Patrick smiling. Nothing so good has ever come to him so easy.

Even the invitation to stay felt unreal in the moment. Tyler distinctly remembers asking Patrick to say it again, because no way was something he wanted so badly falling into his lap without complications. But Patrick *does* want him around, and Tyler has finally stopped waiting for the other shoe to drop.

Things aren't perfect. Patrick may be a great roommate, but they're both willful and opinionated men, accustomed to having things their own way and unused to compromise. Tyler can win any argument he sets his mind to—at least, he could before he met Patrick's equally stubborn ass—and learning when to give ground has been a struggle.

The struggle is worth it for the reasonable rent, and even more worth it when he factors in how desperately he wants to make Patrick happy. But it's a struggle just the same.

Tonight is just such a challenge, though Tyler can't quite believe the disagreement unfolding between them. Here in the moment, as he grows riled and loud and tense, some rational sliver of his mind watches from the periphery, confused at the pointlessness of their argument.

"Because they're *wasteful*," he snaps, an emphatic gesture going wide and nearly knocking over the old-fashioned umbrella propped beside the front door, "and completely unnecessary!"

"I like the way they smell!" Patrick thunders back, expression clouded and eyes narrowed. Despite the size of him—the way he looms over Tyler—there is nothing threatening about his anger.

"Wool ones can be scented! All we need to do is buy some essential oils! Whatever fucking smell you want, I don't care!"

"It's *not the same*!"

Dryer balls. Goddamn *dryer balls*. Tyler cannot, for the life of him, figure out how he's gotten this worked up over whether or not to replace the dryer sheets Patrick usually buys for the laundry room. Every reasonable point is on

Tyler's side. The costs they'll cut if they don't need to buy dryer sheets all the time. The benefit to the environment. The sheer convenience of the thing.

None of these arguments truly matter. Tyler doesn't care this much about laundry.

But he does care about Patrick.

He shuts that thought down, refusing to face it head-on. It's easier, somehow, to focus on how passionate he suddenly feels about convincing his roommate to try the wool dryer balls he bought today.

He's not listening to his own words anymore—doesn't have any idea what Patrick is saying either. Only when silence crashes around them, sudden and startling, does he notice how close they're standing. Somewhere in the last several minutes, Tyler moved away from the door and crowded into Patrick's space. Patrick towers over him, and Tyler stares up with anger—it has to be anger—heating his blood.

Patrick stares back. Equally frozen. Equally silent. Studying Tyler's determined expression.

Then Patrick shatters to life with a breathless, "*Fuck.*" His hands frame Tyler's face, startlingly gentle considering the emotion in his voice—the agitated intensity of their debate—and he leans close.

Somehow despite all of this, the kiss catches Tyler by surprise. His eyes are wide open, his senses spiraling as he tries to catch up. He can't process something so impossible and good, and he stands rigid with shock. With disbelief. With an agony of wanting this to be real, and a rushing heartbeat trying to insist it can't be.

Tyler's stillness must scare Patrick, because too soon he tries to retreat.

No, Tyler thinks frantically. *Don't you dare.* The attempted withdrawal is all it takes for his incredulous heart to finally believe the signals reaching his brain, and he grabs for Patrick in desperate answer. Catches him before he can go far, drags him back down into a renewed and frantic kiss. It's an awkward mess, both of them caught off guard, and Tyler doesn't care.

He closes his eyes. Adjusts his position a little. Patrick also shifts, hands and mouth moving against him, tugging him closer. Easy as that, the kiss is better. It's still eager, still messy, still unexpected—but now all their wavelengths are aligned. Now they're doing this together.

Finally they break apart, in grudging deference to the need for both air and eye contact.

"Oh," Tyler gasps, as he takes in the avalanche of feeling in Patrick's gorgeous brown eyes.

Patrick looks equally upended. "Wow. Yes. Hi."

Laughter follows. Bright, loud, shaking, overwhelmed laughter as both of them recognize the surreal balance of absurdity and heat between them. Tyler feels incandescent, and he's clinging to Patrick as much for balance as for the simple expedient of keeping him close.

"Okay," Patrick says, when both of them manage to quiet. "We can try the wool dryer balls."

Tyler stares for several incredulous heartbeats before bursting once more into helpless laughter.

When Patrick leans in again, the kiss cuts him short but does nothing at all to quell the lightness in Tyler's heart.

An Icy Rain

Theo barely makes it across the threshold before their girlfriend starts laughing.

In Heidi's defense, Theo definitely makes for a disastrous picture right now, drenched past the outer shell of their winter coat, all the way through every layer of clothing beneath.

Theo's jeans have glued themselves to their long legs, the material clinging uncomfortably and sure to get even worse if they don't change before the denim starts to dry. Their hair has plastered to their skin, loose curls directing cascades of icy rainwater down their neck and beneath the collar of their shirt. They look skinny and pathetic and sodden, and it's no wonder Heidi's shoulders are shaking with silent but poorly contained laughter.

"Merry Christmas to you too," Theo mutters, but they can't summon up any heat for the words.

Maybe because there's no heat left in their body.

Technically it's not Christmas yet. Not until tomorrow. But as far as Theo is concerned, Christmas Eve counts, especially when it comes to being irate about unlikely and frankly unacceptable weather.

"Oh god, I'm so sorry," Heidi gasps, finally breaking from her laughter-tinged stillness to help Theo out of the water-logged jacket. "Fucking hell, sweetheart, the state you're in... Did you walk the entire way home in the rain?"

"I forgot my metro card," Theo sulks. "And it wasn't supposed to rain. It's December. Who the hell ever heard of rain in December?" Theo was braced for snow—and lots of it—prepared to trudge through the blizzard that preemptively shut down so many businesses, including the bookstore where they work. But rain? They were not remotely ready for rain. Even now, the sky framing the Christmas tree through the big living room window remains a strange and sickly hue.

The sight is not festive at all, the overall effect not helped by the way this downpour has melted most of the snow.

"Lots of people have rain in December," Heidi says far too reasonably, and Theo stops struggling with the zipper of their hoodie long enough to glare.

"*We* don't," they grumble.

"This is Minnesota, love," Heidi points out, stubbornly failing to intuit that this is not a line of reasoning Theo wants to hear. "We have *all* the weather. Even rain at Christmas sometimes."

"Ugh." Theo finishes fighting with the zipper and drops their sweatshirt to the floor with a wet thump.

Heidi's hands are on Theo's bare arms a second later, firm and steady, rubbing warmth back into shivering limbs. All of Heidi is big and sturdy, her shoulders broad, her smile fond as she watches Theo. She's got the tight coils of her hair tucked into a poofy bun, and she's already washed off the day's makeup, leaving her dark skin so smooth and soft that all Theo wants is to nuzzle in close.

The sight of her ignites a familiar mingling of affection and heat in Theo's chest, and those feelings coalesce into something overwhelmingly bright when Heidi tips their foreheads together.

"You should go change into dry clothes. I'll make cocoa."

Theo follows this advice, even though they don't particularly want Heidi to stop touching them. They collect their rain-heavy sweatshirt from the floor, then put it directly into the empty washing machine along with the rest of their dripping clothes. From there, they dry off with a towel, squeezing as much moisture as possible out of their hair—then quickly change into a pair of pink flannel pajamas. The matched set was intended as a gag gift, but it's become Theo's favorite winter sleepwear. Just snuggling into the soft fabric chases away most of the chill from their bones.

When Theo emerges back into the living room, the sight waiting there warms them the rest of the way through. Heidi has turned on both the electric fireplace and the lights on the enormous tree, dimming the overheads to create a cozy ambiance more befitting the season. Two mugs sit steaming on the coffee table, a mismatched pair in clashing puce and orange. Best of all, Heidi herself sits at one end of the squashy sofa, already lifting one edge of a fuzzy blanket in invitation.

Theo hums a grateful tone and hurries across the room to join her. They drop to the couch in a boneless rush, not bothering to reach for the waiting mug of chocolate just yet. The beverage is tempting, but Heidi's gravity is far more compelling and impossible to resist, and Theo melts against her with an exhausted sigh. Heidi's heat is even more perfect than the cheerful crackle of the artificial fire, or the soft blanket, or the mugs wafting wisps of steam into the quiet air.

Heidi breathes a wordless sound somewhere between a laugh and a purr, and the expression on her face warms Theo all the way to their bare toes. Another moment, and Heidi brushes an indulgent kiss to Theo's forehead, then tucks the blanket more securely around them. Her arm settles around Theo's waist, pressing them close, and Theo sighs at being drawn against their girlfriend's reassuring bulk. Being with Heidi is the easiest thing in the world.

Rain in December or not, Heidi's arms are more than enough to guard against any storm.

Theo burrows in, tucking their face beneath Heidi's jaw and inhaling slowly. Taking in the subtle scents of citrus and fabric softener. Savoring the easy rise and fall of Heidi's chest. Listening to the rhythm of a steady heart beating beneath their ear. Absorbing all this welcome heat, more than enough to chase away the memory of ice from their skin.

"Better?" Heidi murmurs, leaning forward just far enough to collect one of the mugs and put it in Theo's hands.

Theo curls their fingers around smooth ceramic, but the only answer they can manage is a quiet whuff of contentment as their eyes drift shut.

Stubborn Care

There is something aggressively cheerful about the sunlight pouring into the apartment. Or maybe it's the bright scent of spring filling the air from the living room's open windows.

"Would you stop grumbling and *let me take care of you*?" Chris conceals a touch of unwilling amusement beneath an equally honest edge of exasperation. Beni won't appreciate any glimpse of humor in this moment, especially humor at Beni's own expense. The poor guy already feels ridiculous for how he broke his ankle in the first place, no matter how many times Chris points out that there's no shame in failing to spot a long leash— or the tiny dog at the end of it—on a busy downtown sidewalk.

If Beni thinks Chris is laughing at him— even if Chris's amusement stems solely from the mulish frustration with which his partner is reacting to the necessities of convalescence—he will inevitably shut down completely.

And Chris already can't get him to admit when he needs more goddamn painkillers.

What is it about big tough guys that makes them too stubborn to admit the perfectly reasonable limitations of the human body?

"I hate making you wait on me hand-and-foot," Beni rumbles, scowling out the window as though the beautiful weather offends him.

For his part, Chris is relieved the season has finally turned. He's not built for winter. And whether it's an effect of the anemia he's perpetually battling, some shortage of vitamin D, or simple lack of body mass, he's ready to welcome temperatures that don't leave him shivering beneath sweaters and hoodies and winter jackets.

"You're not *making me* do anything." Chris rolls his eyes, torn between his sympathy and his own desire to stop arguing about this. The line between these feelings is remarkably narrow. "Did you resent taking care of me after my surgery?"

"Of course not." Beni's eyes widen with instant affront, and Chris lets the ensuing silence make his point. He crosses his arms and arches an eyebrow, standing directly in front of Beni with his best air of eternal patience. He peers down at Beni on the couch and waits for the trap to close, the net cinching tight and leaving no way for Beni to wiggle out of the inescapable conclusion that he is not, in fact, a burden.

Chris knew going into his top surgery that he was going to have some challenges to contend with while he recovered. The weight restrictions were especially onerous. Amazing how many things a body *can't do* when not allowed to lift anything above five pounds.

If Beni hadn't been there to pick up the slack and keep him company, the process would've been about five hundred times more torturous.

Beni's scowl deepens now, and Chris knows his argument has hit its mark. There's no escaping this unassailable logic. Beni can't worm his way out without acknowledging that he's being a complete hypocrite.

If Chris didn't love him so much, he might toss his hands up in surrender and leave Beni to sulk for a while. A couple hours alone wouldn't do any actual harm. Beni moves around just fine on his crutches, despite doctor's orders to take it easy and keep his ankle elevated.

But Chris's chest clenches with refusal at the thought of leaving Beni to be miserable alone, even for a scant couple of hours. God, Beni looks so uncomfortable even now, with his shoulders tense and his leg resting on multiple pillows atop a rickety stool. He occupies his corner of the couch as though it's holding him hostage, and he still hasn't picked up the mug of coffee Chris brought him.

Just as Chris is beginning to fear Beni will keep arguing with him after all, the tension in those broad shoulders eases into an exhausted slump.

"You're right." The words come out ragged with exhaustion. "I'm being a brat. I'm sorry."

"You don't need to apologize." Chris settles onto the couch beside Beni, mindful not to jostle his leg but unable to resist leaning in close and setting a hand to Beni's chest. He lets his palm rest over the steady heartbeat, absorbing the soft rhythm. "Just let me help, okay? You can tell me to fuck off if I'm too much of a mother hen, but stop beating yourself up about letting me do things for you. We're supposed to be a team."

This last is a deliberate low blow—the exact words Beni used to talk him down from the same guilty sulk a few months ago—and Chris can see just how quickly it works. Beni's expression softens, his mouth twitching at one corner as he slides a hand around Chris's nape.

A gentle tug pulls Chris close, and he braces more of his weight on Beni's muscular chest. Their foreheads bump together, a gesture of affection that sends familiar heat racing through Chris's body. He doesn't make any effort at all to resist leaning in for a kiss, long and slow and just a little bit dirty.

"We good?" Chris asks, when they finally, reluctantly break apart. His face is flushed with heat, and god, if he thought he could do it without causing unintended pain, he would crawl right into Beni's lap and explore other ways to reassure the man he isn't a burden.

"Yeah." Beni's voice comes out a sandpaper rasp of emotion, but his fingers are soft in Chris's hair. "We're good."

Losing Sleep

"Hey. Tristan. Are you awake?"

The question cuts through midnight quiet and drowsy sleep, pulling him out of a pleasant dream. Tristan groans, not at the lost vestiges of fading imagery, but at the fact of being conscious.

He can't tell exactly what time it is, but his eyes feel gritty as he blinks them open to take in the faint strip of hallway light silhouetting his best friend. Alec has always been something of an insomniac—Tristan knows this from years of cohabiting and even more years of closeness—but since starting law school, the guy seems to have sworn off sleep entirely. Impossible to say whether the problem stems from workload, anxiety, or too damn much coffee.

Whatever the cause, this symptom of nocturnal wakeup calls is not Tristan's favorite new trend.

"Go to sleep." He closes his eyes and keeps them closed, making a show of ignoring Alec's disheveled shadow. "It's gotta be two in the goddamn morning."

"Three." Alec's voice sounds infuriatingly alert. "Can I come in?"

Tristan considers refusing. Let Alec find some other distraction. Surely there's someone he could argue with on the internet instead. There must be some other way to expend all the restless energy he's carrying around—one that doesn't involve waking Tristan up in the middle of the night.

But here he is, and Tristan is already huffing a put-upon sigh and scooting back to make room on the mattress. He barely quashes a tired smile when Alec breathes a soft, pleased sound. Light footsteps shuffle across the floor, followed by a tug at the sheet covering Tristan's shoulder.

He still doesn't bother opening his eyes, as Alec slips beneath the covers and curls close. Never shy about demanding physical affection,

Alec has only gotten needier as the semester's progressed. It's a damn good thing they understand one another. Coming from anyone else, Tristan might mistake someone climbing into his bed for an invitation, and that would be intolerably awkward. He might even consider accepting if Alec ever approached with more prurient intentions, though Hell will probably freeze over first.

He raises his arm to let Alec snuggle closer. The concession is grudging, purely because he would rather be asleep. Under normal circumstances he doesn't mind having his space invaded this way. Sometimes it's nice to cuddle with someone who neither wants nor expects anything else. He just wishes it weren't happening two hours before his alarm clock is set to go off.

"Don't suppose I can convince you to just lie quietly and let me sleep," Tristan murmurs, unsurprised when the words earn him a restless squirm of the body in his arms.

"I can try." A sliver of resignation undercuts the soft sincerity, suggesting the attempt won't last long.

Tristan exhales, long and slow. "What's wrong?"

"Nothing."

"You better not have woken me up just to lie to my face."

Alec makes a low sound that might be contrition. Then he's silent for so long Tristan wonders if maybe they *could* just sleep. But a moment later Alec answers more honestly, a floodgate breaking open.

"I keep wondering if law school was the wrong call. It's so fucking hard, and it's way more expensive than I expected—even with my scholarship I'm gonna be drowning in debt by the time I'm done—and at the end of it all... What? I'll get the diploma and the graduation cap, sure, but I still need to pass the Bar. And find a job. And keep it together long enough to start making real money. Why am I doing this to myself?"

"Woah. Okay. First, *breathe*, fucking hell." Tristan waits until he feels Alec inhale, deliberate if shaky, and then says, "Has it occurred to you that three a.m. is maybe a bad time for existential panic?" Or possibly it's the only unavoidable time for existential panic. He lets the point stand.

"I couldn't sleep," Alec protests.

"Yeah. I can see that. But it's the middle of the night. *Everything* seems like a disaster in the middle of the night." Not to mention the weeks of sleep deprivation stacking up to make every hurdle even more daunting.

"You're avoiding the question."

"Technically you didn't ask me a question." Before Alec can follow up, Tristan adds, "Even if you had, I can't make that call. It's not my future we're talking about."

Alec gives an exasperated huff and buries his face against Tristan's shoulder.

"Hey," Tristan says. "What classes do you have tomorrow?"

"CivPro and Contracts."

"Are you doing okay in those classes?"

"Yeah. They're not bad. Why?"

"You're skipping them. And I'm calling in sick to work." He has more sick time stockpiled than he can ever hope to burn through anyway. "We'll order pizza and play video games in pajamas all day. The new Phatal Phantasy came out last Tuesday. I'll download it first thing in the morning."

Alec doesn't say anything for a very long time. When he finally speaks, his voice wobbles suspiciously. "That sounds awesome."

"You should still try to sleep," Tristan says, as gently as possible.

Again on a pronounced delay, Alec asks, "Can I stay here?"

Tristan answers without hesitation. "Of course you can."

In the Crowd

The bar is packed nearly to bursting, which would normally make Cole desperate to be anywhere else.

Not tonight, though. Tonight Cole is delighted at the noisy, enthusiastic throng, because it's not themself they're here for. Cole is here to support their best friend, who stands on that rickety stage *right now*, singing his entire heart out to the adoring audience. Cole hangs back, clear across the room, sitting on the bar stool they haven't left since staking it out before the show. The distance makes it difficult to see the stage with its minimal setup. Amps and speakers, a drum kit, a keyboard, a microphone. Julian's band is small but noisy, and Cole doesn't need a front row seat to know what they look like in the middle of their set.

Even clear at the back of the bar, the press of bodies is oppressive. But Cole does their best to ignore all that and enjoy the gorgeous, gravel-rough tones of Julian's voice soaring over guitar chords and the jangle of the keyboard.

From soulful ballads to raucous anthems, Julian always performs with the same raw power. He sings like he's leaping headfirst into his music, and his intensity hasn't waned in the two decades Cole has known him.

By the end of the set, the room is even more packed, and Cole has begun to seriously consider sneaking away. Julian will understand. He knows Cole gets overwhelmed in tight crowds, probably doesn't expect them to have stayed this long. The band hoped tonight would be a successful show, but this turnout blows every expectation out of the water.

And Cole is delighted, no matter how close they are to making a run for it.

The bartender looks ragged now, at the end of the night. It's the kind of shift that means good money, but it's also been an endless stream of too many people vying for attention at once. More traffic than one server should ever have to field alone, and Cole has made sure to tip exorbitantly for every single refill of the stout they've been slowly nursing all night.

As the crowd finally begins to disburse, Cole stays put. They shut down the inevitable flirtations that come their way, politely but firmly, because they have no interest tonight in cozying up to a stranger, no matter how attractive or charming. Cole has expended every reserve of social energy just keeping their head above water in such a crowded bar. The only person whose company they crave is on that stage packing up the last of the sound equipment, occasionally pausing to shake a hand or sign an autograph.

"You know, there's a tall drink of water at the end of the bar who's been glancing your way all night." The familiar voice, high and lilting, cuts through the noise, and Cole turns a wry look on Angie. Drummer, fashion icon, and gorgeous mountain of a woman who stands a full head taller than Cole's compact frame.

Her red hair looks especially riotous in the patchwork barroom lighting, and her mouth quirks into an encouraging smile.

"You guys done loading the van already?" Cole doesn't make any disingenuous protest about how they could help carry. They're not here to volunteer for someone else's heavy lifting.

"Yes. So? What about your admirer?"

Cole's just curious enough to spare what they hope is a subtle glance across the bar. And the thing is, Angie's right. The man near the door has all the bearing of a big, sweet himbo who hasn't worked up the nerve to introduce himself. One of Cole's many favorite types.

But Cole's got to be in the right mood to enjoy an anonymous hookup, and a night like this isn't anywhere close. They're too spent, and the thought of keeping up the energy for a stranger...

Some other time. Maybe the man will be around a different, quieter night.

"Fuck off with your matchmaking efforts." Julian's cheerful voice cuts in from Cole's other side. A moment later, Julian's powerful arm drapes over Cole's skinny shoulder, tucking them against his side.

Cole instantly relaxes, an involuntary reaction that sends them slumping contentedly into Julian's hug.

"Not my fault people pay attention to a pretty face," Angie fires back brightly.

"Cole came out tonight to support the arts, not score with a stranger." But Julian leans closer a moment later and says in an exaggerated whisper, "Unless you *want* to go home with him. He is unconscionably pretty."

Cole pretends to consider for a long moment before answering. "Nah. I'm too tired for sex." Then they turn their head to look directly into Julian's stubbled and ruggedly handsome face, and say more sincerely, "You guys played great tonight. It was a good show."

Julian grins, wide and warm. "Thanks." Then he glances past Cole and calls, "Night, Angie! Thanks for dealing with the van."

"Goodnight and you're welcome. But also, you owe me."

Then she's vanished into the crowd, so fast Cole doesn't have any chance to add their own goodbye. When Cole looks at Julian again, their friend is watching them with familiar fondness, and just a hint of heat. An answering kindle of feeling warms Cole's stomach, and they consider the possibility. It certainly wouldn't be the first time Cole and Julian have followed up a good show with some private fun of their own.

But Cole really is exhausted, and not in the mood for that kind of fun. And when Julian kisses their temple and asks, "Got any plans for the rest if the night?" Cole already knows what their answer needs to be.

"Falling asleep watching a movie sounds nice. Want to join me?" Cole may not be up for sex—even the laughing, affectionate, easy kind they have with their best friend—but they wouldn't mind letting a long cuddle recharge their low batteries.

Julian's smile goes soft. "Sounds great. Let's get the hell out of here."

Frantic Heat

It's nearly three in the morning when Dale gets home, so he tries to be sneaky—not because he has any reason to conceal how late he's coming in, but because his boyfriend has early meetings tomorrow.

It would be cruel to wake Stephen in the middle of the night, when he'll have to be out the door long before sunrise just to make it to work on time. Hell, if it weren't for Stephen's busy schedule tomorrow, he probably would've joined Dale tonight. The man may be a growly hermit by preference, but he is also the world's sweetest boyfriend. He would tolerate just about any social discomfort for Dale's sake.

And while Dale knows a seven-hour tabletop game will never be Stephen's idea of a good time, he's joined such an endeavor more than once. Letting him get sufficient rest tonight is the least Dale can do under the circumstances.

So Dale moves through the apartment as quietly as he can, leaving his messenger bag on the tiny kitchen table and padding down the hall in stocking feet. He moves even more carefully when he reaches the bedroom, tossing his clothes into the hamper and climbing naked into bed. It's too dark to actually see Stephen, but Dale can picture him with perfect clarity: broad shoulders peeking out from beneath pale sheets; soft hair just long enough to muss against the pillow; silvery stubble dusting a strong jaw.

Even the mental image is enough to make Dale's mouth water, and he wills his libido to shut the fuck up. He's not going to wake Stephen just because Dale is horny and far too caffeinated for sleep.

Dale keeps to his own side of the bed, savoring the nearby warmth of Stephen's body and settling back into his pillow with a sigh. For the barest heartbeat, there is stillness. Dale congratulates himself on not being a pest. He draws in the beginning of a slow breath—

And exhales a startled squeak, as Stephen moves to meet him, covering Dale with his body and taking his mouth in a rough kiss.

Stephen is naked too, and Dale shivers delightedly at the slide of skin, the teasing dance of fingers. He melts for Stephen, wrapping his arms around enormous shoulders just to savor how big Stephen feels on top of him. When he parts his legs, Stephen slides easily and immediately between. A perfect fit. Dale breathes a needy sound, his erection stiffening so fast his head spins, and Stephen ruts against him in answer.

It's deliberate friction—frantic heat—and Dale squirms and arches beneath Stephen's impatient thrusts.

"I was trying to *let you sleep*," he gasps when Stephen stops kissing him in favor of biting at the vulnerable line of Dale's throat. The familiar sting of teeth only heightens the arousal tightening Dale's belly. He tips his head back, offering Stephen a wider canvas. Baring himself for the possessive path of Stephen's mouth along his neck.

He will be wearing the unmistakable bruises of each love bite tomorrow, and he can't wait to glimpse them in the mirror. Anyone who sees him will have some very accurate guesses about what he's been up to.

"I gathered." Stephen's voice rumbles against his pulse point, sending an eager tremble along Dale's spine. "It was sweet of you to try."

Dale's laugh shatters into a shaky moan when Stephen slips a hand between their bodies and finds his cock. There isn't a whole lot of space to maneuver, but with a subtle shift of weight, suddenly Stephen is able to stroke a tight fist along Dale's length. A rush of pleasure bursts across Dale's senses, dizzying and giddy. It lights him up from the inside, and he muffles a cry in the crook of Stephen's shoulder. God, how can something so simple feel so amazing?

"Good?" Stephen asks, voice teasing.

Dale tries very hard to answer coherently, but all that comes out is a helpless, "*Ngh*."

Thank god Stephen knows to take this for encouragement. His grip slides urgently along Dale's shaft, just this side of uncomfortable at first—just the way Dale likes it—then smoother, as the steady slick of precome eases the way. The rhythm is deliberately unpredictable, keeping him on edge as a coil of pleasure builds and builds at the base of his spine. He tries to rut into Stephen's hand, more frantic with each passing second. But the closer Dale gets to release, the more Stephen seems intent on teasing him.

After a torturous and delicious eternity, Stephen goads Dale right to the precipice, and finally—*finally*—lets him tumble over the edge.

It feels like a very long time before Dale's mind stumbles back to reality, and he is delighted to find Stephen still on top of him. Nuzzling at his throat. Rutting idly into the hollow of Dale's hip, apparently with all the patience in the world.

Dale has no idea what time it is now, but he's not going to bother feeling guilty for keeping Stephen awake. He didn't start this.

But oh, he has every intention of finishing it.

When Dale gives a hard push, his physical strength isn't enough to move the muscular weight pinning him down. But Stephen gets with the program quickly, rolling obediently onto his back as Dale kicks aside the bedclothes and scrambles to follow. He doesn't need light to do this. He doesn't need to see Stephen in the darkness, when it's so easy to navigate by touch, easing farther down the bed and kneeling between Stephen's legs.

A new rush of anticipation thrills through him, and Dale grins when he says, "My turn."

Then, for a very long while, he doesn't say anything at all.

Longer Distance

When Andrea opens her eyes, bleary and disoriented, the first thing her sleep-addled senses register is the face of her digital alarm clock. It sits in its place on the bedside table, glaring and familiar. The numbers cut through the otherwise total darkness, ruby red and proclaiming the hour.

Three o'clock. Nowhere near morning. Why the hell is she awake at three a.m., when usually she sleeps all the way through sunrise?

A quiet buzz rattles the silence, startling her, though not enough to shake off the stubborn vestiges of sleep. Her phone. It's vibrating in the shadows just beyond the alarm clock, screen-side down. Andrea's aim is a little off when she reaches for it by sound alone.

The buzzing continues—*Silent mode my ass*, she thinks—and her second wild grope across the darkness finally lands on the smooth bamboo cover. She blinks away the worst of the sleep from her eyes and drags the phone toward her without disconnecting the charging cable.

Kelly's name lights up the screen, bright in the pitch darkness. The fact that her fiancé is calling at three in the morning from halfway around the globe is enough to knock Andrea wide awake in an instant. Any lingering grogginess evaporates, replaced by alert attention as she swipes her thumb across the bottom of the screen.

"Babe? Everything okay?"

"Why wouldn't it be?" Kelly asks. She sounds unconcerned, if slightly perplex. "And why does your voice sound like half-dry cement?"

Andrea snorts at the remarkably apt description. Her voice *feels* like cement, dragged up from sleep with no warning. Her mind might be abruptly and frantically awake, but her throat is still graveled and tired and grudging when she speaks.

"Sweetheart," she groans, rubbing the bridge of her nose and squeezing her eyes tightly shut.

"God damn it, I fucked up the time difference."

"You fucked up the time difference," Andrea agrees wryly. Relief is careening through her though, and it softens the roughest edges of her tone.

"Fuck," Kelly breathes, sheepishness tingeing the word. "I'm so sorry. I swear I tried to calculate it right. I must've gone the wrong direction."

"It's okay," Andrea murmurs. It really is. Now that she isn't on the cusp of worried panic, she's just glad to hear her fiancé's voice. It's been nearly two weeks with Kelly an ocean away and out of reach—a business trip that bodes well for the prospect of a big promotion on the horizon—but neither of them is accustomed to being apart so long, and sure as hell not with such a vast distance sprawling between them.

"It's not okay," Kelly says. There's no sound to suggest movement, but Andrea can picture Kelly shaking her head stubbornly, dark curls bouncing in a warm sunset. "Go back to sleep. I'll call you in a few hours."

"That'll be *your* middle of the night," Andrea counters reasonably. At least, she's mostly sure that's the case. She isn't great with time zones herself, or basic math, or anything that requires more than a small modicum of brain power at this unreasonable time of night.

"Yeah, but you didn't sign up for a midnight wakeup call."

"Talk to me anyway." Andrea does not point out that it's not technically midnight. Arguing that hey, no, actually it's three a.m., isn't likely to make Kelly feel any better about waking her. But Andrea is fully conscious now, and painfully aware of how empty her bed is. She glances at Kelly's unused pillow, and the sudden ricochet of longing in her chest is so powerful she might actually cry if Kelly hangs up. With difficulty, she smoothes her tone into something brighter—something less lovelorn and more cheerful—and asks, "What did you want to tell me?"

"Nothing," Kelly admits, and Andrea can hear a smile through the rueful tone. Kelly's voice is always gorgeous—warm and rich and almost tenor-deep—but it's loveliest when she's smiling. "I just missed you."

Andrea laughs, and if a little too much feeling sneaks into the sound, that's fine. Kelly will be abroad for another full week. Three weeks for the trip in total. It's the longest they've ever been apart, and more than once Andrea has almost caught herself begging Kelly to cut the trip short somehow. It's imperfect consolation, hearing Kelly admit she called just to hear Andrea's voice, but it heats a much-needed ember in her chest just the same.

"I miss you too." Andrea slumps back down, setting the phone beside her pillow and finding a comfortable position on her back. The ceiling is all deep shadows above her, the room cool and silent, the mattress soft beneath her weight. "Tell me about your day."

"You better not fall asleep during my story," Kelly says. Fond amusement makes the words sparkle and shine.

"No promises." Andrea punctuates the statement with an involuntary yawn. She tugs the blankets up to her chin and breathes a soft purr of contentment. She would prefer to have Kelly touchable and here beside her, of course. But she's not going to complain about the voice in her ear, already embarking on a complicated tale about double-booked meeting rooms and business conference intrigues.

Calming further every second, Andrea settles more comfortably into her pillow. She

floats on the soothing tide of her fiancé's words,
and lets herself drift away.

Musical Notes

Del doesn't immediately announce himself when he steps outside, though he's confident Victor hears him approach. Never mind the creak of the screen door ushering him into the autumn-cool night. Victor's uncanny vigilance—born of a past he doesn't like to talk about—makes it unlikely Del could ever sneak up on him.

But whether Victor notices Del's presence or not, his fingers keep moving over the guitar, continuing the melody that compelled Del out here in the first place.

It's something Victor wrote himself. Del would swear to it, though he'd be hard pressed to explain how he knows. There's something honest and open in every swift note— something almost wistful in the crescendo that rises gradually to drown out the murmur of frogs and crickets in the yard. Del watches

Victor's broad back and absorbs the heartfelt meandering of the tune.

He wonders what it means. Victor always laughs when asked such direct questions about his music, just shrugs and averts his eyes and says it's only a song. But Del knows music. No one crafts something this beautiful without a mountain of feeling behind it.

Eventually the song ends, trembling to a quiet stop.

Silence holds awhile before Victor says, "You gonna sit down or not?"

Del laughs and lets the screen door clatter shut behind him, then crosses to the edge of the wide deck and folds himself down beside Victor. Del's feet don't quite reach the ground when he kicks them over the edge, and he swings them idly in the open air. Beside him, Victor maintains a more perfect stillness. Just one more difference between them. Del's restless energy to Victor's perpetual calm. Del's clumsy chaos to Victor's easy elegance. Del's beanpole frame to Victor's short, stocky build.

When Del glances sideways, he finds rough, handsome features softened by moonlight. The silver scattered through Victor's hair and beard reflects the dim light, and his eyes seem almost to glow when he turns and meets Del's perusal.

"I bet Steve fifty bucks that you wouldn't even make it to nine o'clock before sneaking out here." Del hopes his impish tone will conceal how caught-out he feels, staring at Victor with no apparent cause.

Victor's fond smile is barely visible in the shadows, but it's audible in his voice. "Some friend you are."

Del grins. "I got it right, didn't I? You should be happy for me. I'm leaving this party fifty bucks richer than when I arrived."

"Then yes," Victor deadpans. "I'm delighted for you."

Del huffs a sound suspiciously like a giggle and scoots closer, letting his head tip down onto Victor's shoulder. It feels like such a dangerous thing to do. Like he's showing too much of his heart.

What if, for all the times Del has done this before, Victor finally sees through him and reads something more complicated beneath the gesture?

Del's brain can't even conjure theoretical consequences. He's been carrying this torch for so long, he's lost all sense of proportion. Maybe Victor finding out would be an absolute catastrophe. Maybe it would be a complete non-event, and they could continue on as though nothing's changed. Maybe it would be the best thing in the world.

Since he has no idea how the chips will fall, Del stubbornly continues to play it safe. He allows himself this wordless intimacy and nothing more. No further truth. And all the while, he harbors desperate contradictory hopes.

"I don't like crowds," Victor says, breathing the words like a confession.

"I know." Del matches his low tone. "It's okay."

"Steve might take it personally that we both abandoned his graduation party less than an hour after arriving."

"Steve's had six graduation parties," Del retorts. "If he's going to keep racking up esoteric degrees, he doesn't get to be angry at us for multitasking."

"Multitasking?" Victor says, and Del can't decide if he sounds amused or incredulous. Maybe both. "Is that what we're calling this?"

"Sure," Del says with exaggerated cheer. "You're playing your guitar, and I'm listening to you play. How is that not multitasking?"

"Mmm," Victor murmurs, thoroughly noncommittal. But he turns his head and presses a kiss to Del's hair, and the gesture melts Del's heart in the best and worst ways.

He loves this man so much it makes his head spin.

"Is it a new song?" Del asks, desperately hoping Victor reads something besides naked yearning in his voice.

"Yes."

"Will you play it for me again?"

He closes his eyes as Victor starts at the beginning, listening with all his senses alert. Del knows he's making it more difficult to play, leaning against Victor like this, but Victor doesn't protest. The ebb and rush of shimmering notes sounds as masterful and easy as any music the man's ever played. God, Victor is such a gorgeous adept. Del pictures blunt fingers sliding along the neck of the guitar to shape the chords. He pictures Victor's other hand alternately plucking and strumming as the composition demands.

Eventually, the notes taper to the same lulling conclusion Del heard when he stepped out onto the deck. His chest feels so full he aches, unsure how his body can possibly contain this much affection without exploding. He keeps his eyes closed, keeps his breathing steady by force of will.

"That's beautiful." And then, even though he has no reason to expect a different answer from every other time, Del asks, "What's it about?"

For a long while Victor *doesn't* answer. Anticipation holds taut and off-balance, poised in an indecipherable eternity. Del falls into absolute stillness. He doesn't consciously intend to hold his breath; it's just that he's forgotten how his lungs work.

When Victor finally speaks, his one-word reply rumbles with gravel.

"It's about you," he says.

And Del finally remembers how to breathe.

Sleeping In

Morgan is disoriented when she first wakes, blinking up at a ceiling that looks too smooth to belong in her bedroom, startled by a slant of sunlight cutting the wrong direction through the window. The pillow doesn't smell quite right either, soft with lavender and a hint of citrus when her own laundry only ever has a plain, clean dryer-sheet smell.

By the time she finishes turning her head to take in more of her surroundings, she has already remembered enough of last night to stop being confused. The memories are a little hazy, pleasant and noisy and tipsy all at once. Morgan didn't have much to drink, but it never takes much to get her wobbling. A couple of beers and a single shot, before switching over to soda like the lightweight she is. But when she calls up the contours of her night out—her best friend at her side almost every moment of the evening—the images come easily enough through the distortion of a thankfully mild hangover.

She isn't surprised to finish rolling onto her side and discover Leah in the bed beside her, sleeping in a clumsy sprawl with one side of her face squashed into the pillow. Leah is beautiful even like this, a fact on which Morgan reflects with wry fondness. Dark eyelashes brush long and delicate over the deep brown of an excessively sharp cheekbone. Her soft lips are parted, stained an uneven maroon from last night's makeup, and there's still a suggestion of glitter on her eyelid. Her long neck and smooth shoulder sweep scandalously from the loose neckline of the oversized t-shirt she slept in.

If Morgan were the sort to entertain feelings of a romantic nature, she suspects she would find herself inevitably and powerfully smitten with her best friend. As it is, she has occasionally spared a wistful thought of *What If.* She adores Leah in her own complicated way. She would certainly fool around with Leah if such an invitation were offered with no strings attached.

But Morgan knows just how bad an idea that would be for them. Leah has never been the sort to keep sex and romance in separate compartments of her brain, so those are lines she and Morgan will never cross.

Morgan doesn't mind. She doesn't especially care about sex one way or the other, but she cares very much about Leah. And now, easy and comfortable in her best friend's bed, Morgan drapes a protective arm around Leah and burrows in close. Leah's breath ghosts across her jaw, slow and steady with sleep. A moment later, there is the smallest shift of Leah's weight on the mattress as, without waking, she curls even closer and tucks her head beneath Morgan's chin.

"Sap," Morgan murmurs, and can't decide if she means her unconscious friend or her own ridiculous and affectionate heart.

"Takes one to know one," Leah retorts, the words blurry with sleep for all that they prove she is more awake than Morgan realized. There's a smile in the syllables, perfectly audible despite the fact that Morgan can't actually see Leah's face to confirm. And a moment later, when Leah wraps an arm tightly around her waist and tugs her close, Morgan's own mouth tilts into a wide grin.

"Good morning," Morgan says.

"Mmm," Leah breathes noncommittally.

Morgan huffs an exasperated sound, but she doesn't push. Leah did drink more than her last night. If Morgan is waking with this strange, fuzzy not-quite-hangover setting the world off balance, she can only imagine how Leah must be feeling. The fact that Leah still seems determined to stay in bed and hide from the encroaching sunlight, strongly suggests she's got a headache at the very least. Normally Leah is an egregiously cheerful early riser. She doesn't even need coffee to face the day—something to which Morgan absolutely cannot relate.

Without coffee, a person may as well sleep until noon as far as Morgan is concerned.

Thank god she spends so much time in this apartment that Leah keeps a coffee maker and a constant supply of decent grounds on hand. Even Leah will probably partake of a cup if Morgan brews a pot today.

"How are you feeling?" Morgan asks, teasing her fingertips along Leah's scalp.

"Mmm," is all Leah says again.

Still not much to go on. But then, Morgan feels no urgency to get up and start the day either. The coffee can wait. She's far too content right where she is. She's not going to rush out of this comfortable bed, or prematurely surrender the warm cuddles she is enjoying so much.

Eventually restlessness rises, inevitable as the tide.

"Want me to get you some water?" Morgan offers, ducking to press a kiss to the crown of Leah's head. "Painkillers? Breakfast?"

"No," Leah mumbles, mouth so soft it tickles where her lips brush against the hollow of Morgan's throat. "Stay here."

"All right." Morgan soothes a hand down Leah's back, all along the sweep of her spine. "Get some more sleep, then. I'll stay."

"Mmm," Leah sighs once more. This time the sound carries unmistakable contentment.

Morgan closes her eyes and lets herself drift.

At the Beach

Beyond the shade cast by an enormous and excessively colorful beach umbrella, the sun shines down so brightly that it's physically painful. It doesn't help that the white sand and rolling waves reflect all that light in too many directions at once. Add the fact that Billy is prone to nasty sunburns if he so much as *looks* at a clear blue sky, and he's feeling pretty foolish about agreeing to this particular venture.

But Sam asked him to come. Sam smiled that beautiful smile—the one that deepens the creases at the corners of his eyes and makes him look like a devilish imp—and Billy couldn't bring himself to refuse. Besides, on a practical level, surely it would've been a faux pas to turn down his very first invitation to vacation with his boyfriend's family.

Though it's probably not much less of a faux pas to sit here alone, while everyone else is out laughing and swimming and chasing each other in the surf.

At least Billy has the consolation that he made a good initial impression. Sam's siblings are all charmingly exuberant, Sam's nieces are tiny little capsules of chaos, and Billy overheard Sam's parents whispering about what a sweet young man he is. Hopefully no one has even noticed that he's hiding alone beneath the umbrella, wishing he had brought a book down to the beach with him. He doesn't even have his phone to help distract him. The damn thing won't work when it overheats, and even in the shade it's hot as hell today.

Billy has mostly managed to keep track of Sam across the sand, despite the distance and the over-crowded beach. The man's average height doesn't much help, but the premature shock of white hair sure stands out. As far as Billy can tell, Sam's playing a game of tag with his nieces, though with everyone cackling and changing direction at abrupt intervals, Billy has no idea who's winning.

He does his best to quell the sudden surge of feeling *left out.* For fuck's sake, he knew from the start that this was the only possible way the day could go. And he came anyway. He made a conscious choice. He refuses to be so petulant as to resent the consequences of his actions.

He's exerting so much energy trying to talk himself out of a looming sulk that it takes him a moment to realize Sam is moving toward him up the beach.

With every step closer, Sam is easier to track through the throng of beachgoers, and Billy's breath hitches. His belly flutters with familiar longing, and he wonders how Sam can still have such a powerful impact on him after more than a year together. Surely some of the novelty should have worn off by now. Surely Billy shouldn't feel like he's reverted to a randy teenager just because he's caught a glimpse of his boyfriend shirtless from forty feet away.

But goddamn, Sam looks so good. His dark swim trunks are just wet enough from the water to cling to his big thighs. Even better, his broad torso glints where ocean spray has yet to evaporate from the thick dusting of chest hair. His whole muscular frame moves with the comfortable pace of a man who is perfectly at ease in his own skin.

Billy folds his legs toward his chest, wrapping his arms around them as he bites down hard on his lower lip.

"You okay, babe?" Sam murmurs as he ducks beneath the umbrella and sits on the blanket beside Billy. He doesn't bother reaching for a towel, clearly content to let the heavy heat finish drying his skin.

Billy is shirtless too—a state of being that still feels strange in public, even two years since his top surgery—and the lack of fabric does nothing to make him feel cooler in the stifling air. Still, a pleased smile flickers at the corner of his mouth when he spots Sam's leisurely gaze sliding along the full length of his body, brazen and appreciative.

Billy doesn't feel particularly sexy in his own bright floral shorts and an ungodly quantity of sunscreen, but it's nice to know he's not the only one enjoying the view.

"I'm okay." He leans in and bumps his shoulder against Sam's arm. "Just didn't really think the whole *beach* thing through."

Sam's eyes sparkle with fondness and understanding. "Not your kind of place?"

Billy cracks a sheepish grin. "Not really, no."

"Mmm." Sam scoots closer, dropping a kiss to the corner of Billy's mouth and then draping an arm across his shoulders despite the heat. His skin is faintly sticky from the saltwater. "I'll have to make it up to you later."

"Yeah?" Billy's pulse picks up, bright and interested. "How you planning to do that?"

"You'll have to wait and find out." There's a delicious rumble of promise beneath the words, and a shimmer of mischief in Sam's eyes. "But I bet we can make a strategic retreat pretty soon. I did my part to wear the little ones out, and my folks always insist on napping before dinner anyway."

Billy imagines running away, just the two of them, back to the resort at the end of the beach. Back to their room, where they can tuck themselves away and have at least a couple hours just the two of them.

"Okay," he breathes, snuggling in closer and dropping his head to Sam's shoulder with a pleased sigh. "I can wait."

A Messy Question

"Have you ever been in love?"

The question sets Kara off into a choking spasm, as she tries to swallow her drink and ends up with a mouthful of stout down the wrong tube. She gasps and coughs, hiding her face in the crook of her elbow as she clears her airway—then keeps right on coughing for several seconds that seem to stretch out into forever. She's dimly aware of her best friend's open palm thumping her hard between the shoulder blades, in a sweet but unproductive effort to help.

"Sorry, sorry." Joan sounds guilty and chagrined, her whole broad frame folded toward Kara as she shifts from pounding on Kara's back to rubbing soothing circles in the same spot. The heat of her touch ignites a familiar contradiction beneath Kara's skin, steady calm and greedy tension in equal parts.

Kara's body has no idea how to respond to Joan, and the stubborn yearning in her chest only exacerbates a problem she's been struggling with for years.

"I'm okay," Kara lies. Their server—squat and somber and cute, with a sea-foam green undercut that jibes perfectly with the bar's whimsical nautical theme—spares her a worried glance on the way past the narrow table, but doesn't stop to ask if she's okay. Kara indulges a moment of wistful disappointment, because she's pretty sure the server was flirting with her before, and that's probably going to stop now that they've seen what a disaster she actually is.

She takes a more careful sip of her beer, swallowing successfully this time. The cool drink goes down smoothly, helping to soothe her angry throat. Joan remains a muddled presence in Kara's peripheral vision—a silhouette offering up only the blurriest suggestion of brown skin and bright red sweater—thanks to an involuntary sheen of tears. Kara blinks the moisture away easily enough and gives her head a rueful shake.

Joan's hand stays at her back, a solid presence, and Kara is not the slightest bit tempted to shake it off.

"Yes, I've been in love," she says, because if Joan has broached the subject in the first place, then she's damn sure going to be curious enough to circle back. Especially after eliciting such a dramatic response. Joan is a big, sweet teddy bear, but she's also nosy as hell, and there's no way she lets this drop. Kara's only hope of sidestepping a deeper interrogation is to answer gamely, like the question isn't a big deal.

Like she hasn't been in love with her best friend for longer than she ever intends to admit.

"Yeah?" Joan leans closer, and Kara blinks her vision clear just in time to watch thick eyebrows rising high on Joan's forehead. A conspiratorial smile spreads across Joan's face, making her eyes crinkle at the corners. "Anyone I know?"

It takes reserves of poise that Kara didn't realize she possessed, just to shrug and give Joan a breezy smile. "Probably. Not that I'm going to tell you." She's never seriously dated anyone, but maybe the lack of obvious contenders will help dampen the discussion.

Joan's hand withdraws, and Kara immediately misses the contact, even as Joan gives her shoulder an affronted shove. "Kara, what the hell? I tell *you* everything."

It's true. Joan has no filter at all—she's a woman who speaks every fleeting thought to cross her mind—which is how Kara knows her best friend has never once looked at her with anything like romantic speculation.

Kara shrugs. "It's not that big a deal," she lies again, not sounding quite so breezy this time, but still close enough to deflect and obfuscate how fraught this conversation suddenly feels. "Nothing ever happened. Nothing's *going* to happen. You're not missing out on any actual gossip."

"How do you know nothing will happen?" Joan presses stubbornly, bumping her shoulder against Kara's in a show of encouragement that only makes the absurdity of the situation more apparent.

"Who says I'm still in love with them?" Kara counters, and it comes out sounding brattier than she intends. But there's no way in hell she's going to admit she's still in over her head, any more than she's willing to admit to falling for Joan in the first place.

"Oh." Joan subsides and seems to give this question serious consideration. A moment later, she reaches out to reclaim her lager, giving Kara a considering look. "*Are you* still in love with them?"

Something about the way she asks—earnest and sheepish, with her forehead scrunched and her eyes piercingly intense—makes Kara laugh despite the thrum of cornered adrenaline. She's staring like Kara is a puzzle that Joan's genuinely perplexed at her inability to solve.

But then, it's not as though Kara usually makes herself this opaque, deliberately or otherwise. Other than this huge and inconvenient truth, she's never kept secrets from Joan.

Kara's smile, when she finally makes herself look directly at her best friend, is only a little melancholy. "It doesn't matter," she says, the twinge in her chest so familiar that it barely hurts. "They're not interested. Which is fine. Romance isn't the only way to love someone."

"Well, yeah." Joan leans closer, and Kara's smile shifts a little brighter, a little more genuine. "But you're amazing. You deserve good things."

Kara huffs, exasperated and wry and full of helpless affection.

"It's okay," she insists, more emphatically this time. "I have lots of good things."

Joan hums in agreement, throws an arm over Kara's shoulder, and clinks their glasses together. "Damn right you do."

She leaves her arm there, and Kara leans into her, savoring Joan's warmth and—just for a moment—simply letting herself exist.

Rooftop Interlude

"We're definitely not supposed to be up here," Drake says, though he doesn't so much as tug on Jon's hand to try and slow his husband down. There's nothing particularly unsafe about the roof of their apartment building. It's just that the door usually stays locked, and tenants aren't supposed to have access. "Where'd you get the key, anyway?"

Jon tosses the quickest grin over his shoulder, his expression wild and lovely in the glow of a sunset that is just beginning. The flashlight in Jon's free hand suggests they're likely to be up here for quite some time.

"I called in a favor," Jon answers, gaze focusing forward as he tugs Drake the long way around some kind of utility box. "Don't tell me you'd rather spend our anniversary in a root cellar."

"No." Drake doesn't bother reining in the ridiculous smile that spreads across his face at his husband's playful tone. "But maybe somewhere *on the ground*."

"Boring," Jon retorts, giving a dismissive wave of his flashlight hand. "Don't pass judgment until we get there, okay? Trust me."

"I do," Drake says, soft and fond. He gives Jon's fingers a squeeze and then falls quiet, perfectly willing to let himself be guided across a surprisingly clean rooftop. He's careful of his footing, as Jon tugs him past chimney stacks and water pipes and one particularly massive structure that must have something to do with the elevator.

It's an enormous building, but Drake's never been quite so aware of it as he is now, slowly crossing what feels like an entire city block, dozens of stories up from ground level.

By the time they reach their destination, they're starting to run out of roof and Drake has begun to worry that Jon intends to teach him parkour.

Then they round one last stodgy brick outcropping, and Jon pulls him to a stop with a breathy, "*Here*."

Drake inhales sharply, eyes drawn irresistibly out across a stunning horizon. Their apartment building stands tall enough above its neighbors that nothing blocks the perfect view of the harbor far below. Sunlight glints warm and striking across waves and ships' hulls and the sweep of city along the shore. Faint clouds drift across an increasingly pink sky, and everything feels somehow close and intimate, despite being a vast distance away.

"Holy fuck," Drake gasps. And then his gaze cuts downward from the horizon, and he realizes the view isn't the only thing Jon brought him up here for. A soft blanket and several squashy pillows have been positioned on a shallow slant of roof, perfect for watching the sunset—or for stargazing. A plastic crate draped with fabric has been pressed into service as a picnic basket, and a soft-sided cooler holds what looks like a bottle of champagne.

The whole arrangement is set far enough back from the edge to quell any nervousness Drake might harbor about being so high above the ground. And though a chilly wind cuts past them now and then, Drake's leather jacket is barrier enough to keep him warm. No wonder

Jon wore one of his winter coats to help shield his lanky frame though. Once the sun goes down, it's going to be a good thing they've got at least one blanket to snuggle up with.

"What do you think?" Jon asks, when Drake stays silent too long.

Drake shakes off the rush of awe and tugs Jon against his chest. He doesn't quite close the distance—doesn't give in to the nearly overpowering urge to claim a kiss—contenting himself instead with a close study of Jon's lovely face, round and bright and impish.

Jon's umber-dark eyes search Drake as though for reassurances he can't possibly need. His long lashes, tan skin, high cheekbones, dimpled chin—all of these details paint the portrait of a man Drake loves so much he sometimes doesn't know what to do with this surplus of emotion. It speeds through his broad chest like a second necessary heartbeat, taking Drake's breath away and leaving him helpless in the perfect spotlight of Jon's fixed attention.

Distracted as he is by his husband's hopeful smile, Drake takes an extra moment to remember that Jon asked him a question—and a moment more beyond that to remember what it was, so he can actually answer.

"I think this is beautiful," Drake says. *I think* you're *beautiful*, he thinks, but does not say aloud. No matter how true it is, Jon always shies from the words and finds some way to deflect. Too self-conscious to accept such earnest praise without showing distress. So Drake doesn't push his luck, instead tipping his forehead to rest against Jon's and murmuring a soft, "Thank you, love. Happy anniversary."

Jon leans in—wraps his arms across Drake's shoulders—and his answering smile shines wide and warm as the sky.

On a Mission

"Okay, but does it really need to be this precise doll?" Alex knows exasperation is creeping into their voice, alongside the frazzled edge that's been there since this conversation began, but there's no reining it in now. They feel only a faint twinge of guilt for having their phone on its speaker setting in public. Their earbuds are long dead, and at seven o'clock in the morning there's not a soul to be seen within five aisles in any direction.

No one is shopping for toys at this hour on a weekday.

No one except Alex, anyway, and they would desperately love to be anywhere but here.

They stare at the wall of toys in dull despair. Dozens upon dozens of different designs, brands, characters, and not one of them is what Alex actually needs.

It's not just a matter of their gaze missing the correct tiny plastic figure amid the overwhelming array of options. They've already asked an employee, in case their eyes simply glazed past what they're looking for beneath the garish overhead fluorescents. No luck. Out of stock.

Fuck.

"Yes, love. It really needs to be this doll." Elma sounds perfectly at ease. Her smooth, rich tenor tones come out tinny through the phone speaker. Alex can picture her offering a maddeningly amused smile, sipping from a whimsical coffee mug in one hand while holding the phone in a loose grip in the other. Leaning against the counter in her favorite flannel pajamas and a faded bath robe, filling the little kitchen so easily with the vibrant force of her personality.

Which is exactly where Alex would be, if they hadn't volunteered for this awful errand. They could be at home right now, sharing Elma's coffee. Maybe sharing other things. It could have been a lazy morning with wakeup sex and breakfast, no need at all to put on clothes and brave a disagreeable winter day just to visit a mall halfway across the city.

Instead, Alex is standing in a toy aisle—*voluntarily,* god help them—failing at the only task they need to accomplish today, and the entire reason they're here.

"What about same brand, different doll?" Alex tries, already knowing what the answer will be. Surely it's a reasonable strategy to consider, at least. There are six other dolls from the same lineup, arrayed across the topmost shelf and nearly out of reach for someone of Alex's height. What if they bought all six? Expensive and impractical, but surely a tolerable consolation prize, even for a child prone to hyperfixation.

"Mint-Sprinkle Stardust is his favorite character." Elma still sounds infuriatingly unharried, which isn't fair when Alex can feel themself approaching the edge of panic. Over a toy. God damn it. "It's okay if you can't find one today. The party's not for another week. We can try a different mall."

"But I said I would take care of it." Alex's eyes track the shelves beyond the dolls now. There are tiny basketball hoops with wide bases and plastic nets. Racetracks with miniature cars. Shiny horses in portable stables. Spaceships from some franchise Alex is only peripherally familiar with, something to do with black holes and time travel.

The toy aisle is awash in jarring splashes of color and garish fonts, and none of it is what Alex needs.

They wanted to do this right. It's the first time since they and Elma officially became a couple that there's been a family gathering to attend. Elma's nephew may only be seven, but Alex has their heart set on making a good impression anyway, on both the sprout and on Elma's sister. Showing up with the wrong toy definitely won't achieve that outcome.

"I can hear you overthinking this." Elma's voice interrupts Alex's spiral with a firm steadiness that will not be denied. "Breathe, love. We'll find the doll another day. And if we don't, we'll choose something else. Whether he likes his present or not, he's going to like *you* just fine. And so will the rest of my family."

"Promise?" Alex tries to sound cheeky, but too much honesty sneaks into the question. There's no denying that their more anxious instincts have taken the wheel, dragging them along a familiar path of self-doubt and nerves, and leaving them on unsteady ground. Rationally, they know these fears are ridiculous. Of course Elma's family will like them just fine. Elma's family are not assholes, and Alex is personable and friendly.

Besides, Elma loves Alex. That should be enough.

But the more dubious voice in Alex's head is difficult to shut down, and they're grateful when Elma answers with unrelenting certainty.

"I promise," she murmurs, projecting all the confidence Alex is so desperate to feel. She sounds so fierce and sincere that even Alex's doubts loosen their stranglehold, and the ground feels suddenly more sturdy beneath their feet.

"Okay. I believe you."

"Good. Now *come home*. Breakfast is waiting."

Alex draws a slow breath. Another. Leveling themselves out with the sound of Elma's voice, her reassuring presence on the other end of the line. Alex didn't mean to close their eyes, but when they finally blink again—when they allow awareness of their surroundings back in—it's a little easier to tune out the visual chaos of information spread along the toy aisle.

They turn toward the exit and move with calmer purpose. "I'm on my way."

Midnight

Midnight always does strange things to Lou's head.

And okay, maybe more than just her head. She acknowledges this to herself, as she braces both arms behind her on the hood of her car, the metal just shy of uncomfortably warm beneath her palms. The heat is a welcome point of contact—a contrast to the stinging winter chill and biting wind.

Above her, a dizzy swathe of sky stretches all the way into eternity, barely touched by light pollution from her tiny mosquito-bite of a hometown. The streetlight behind her burned out months ago, and the cozy shop fronts are all darkened windows for the night. When she tips her gaze up and up, she gets a feeling almost like vertigo from the endless stars and the bright wedge of moon. Even after returning her attention to the sprawling horizon, the world doesn't seem quite real.

Midnight does strange things to her heart too, is the problem. It makes her feel shaky. Unsure. Needy. Lonely. It leaves her vulnerable to longings that she normally does a better job of ignoring.

The darkness and quiet linger, strange and uncanny. The late hour feels disconnected from everything, including tomorrow's consequences. Even the moon looks surreal, enormous at the edge of the treetops to Lou's left, cool light over a thin sheen of snow and a lake covered in ice. There's supposed to be a storm coming, but so far Lou sees no sign of it in the perfectly clear sky.

A car door slams somewhere behind her, and even distracted as she is, she wonders how she could've missed the sound of her best friend's junker pulling into the parking lot. Lou's car faces the lake at the very edge of the lot, and her perch on the warm hood has long since turned into a careless slouch. She finally shoves her hands into her coat pockets, shivering beneath her layers.

It's midnight in January. Even bundled up against the cold, this isn't exactly a pleasant night to be loitering outdoors.

"What'd you want to tell me that you couldn't just say over the phone?" Jackie's voice, wry and incredulous, cuts through the cold, warming Lou all the way through. "Christ, dude, it's freezing out here."

Lou snorts at the understatement and finally turns to look over her shoulder. Jackie has been her closest friend for years, and Lou still grins like a fool at the sight of her. She stands bundled even more heavily than Lou, thick jacket swaddling her all the way down to the knees, her neck wrapped in a puffy blue scarf. Jackie's ridiculous knit hat sits lopsided on her head, one tassel missing and the purple stripes looking black and white in the darkness. Her round face bears a scowl that makes it clear just how much she hates the cold, and her eyes are enormous behind thick glasses.

Her stocky frame looks even broader beneath all those layers of sweatshirt and jacket and massive scarf. A couple of dark curls sneak out from beneath the hat, framing her stern features with a softer touch.

Beautiful.

When Jackie reaches her side, Lou does her best to sound nonchalant as she shrugs and says, "Get up here already, if you're so cold. Me and my car will keep you warm." Her heart is beating so rapidly that her chest aches, but it's a happy sort of panic. A delight that Jackie is here. Maybe tonight will finally be the night Lou opens her mouth and speaks even a fragment of how she feels. Maybe she'll kiss Jackie tonight. Maybe Jackie will kiss her back.

Midnight doesn't just make her yearn. It makes her reckless, and she stares as Jackie finally reaches the front of her little sports car and hops onto the hood beside Lou. The car rocks as Jackie settles beside her, and Lou wastes no time before squirming in against her best friend's side.

Jackie huffs an exasperated breath, but she raises her arm without protest and tucks Lou closer.

The physical warmth is nice, but it's the softer sense of closeness that truly does Lou in. Despite the fact that they've done this hundreds of times, her heart races anyway, just like it always has. Just like it does every time Jackie touches her, ever since Lou figured out the flutter Jackie inspires in her belly has nothing to do with friendship. God, Lou is a wreck. She makes herself stare out across the lake and wills her breathing steady.

"So?" Jackie gives her a deliberate squeeze, which is probably intended to be reassuring but only makes Lou's heart pound faster. "I'm here. What are we talking about?"

Right. Because Lou summoned her best friend out here in the middle of the night for a purpose. And she can't just shrug and say *Nothing* now that Jackie is here. She's called her own bluff. Or maybe Jackie's the one calling her bluff, showing up like this in the middle of the night, while what passes for downtown stands silent and empty behind them.

The impossible quiet of a winter night surrounds them, muffled by snow and occasionally jostled by a thready gust of wind.

Lou takes a long, slow breath and wraps her arms around Jackie's thick waist, the down-stuffed jacket squashing beneath her embrace and letting her feel Jackie's sturdy bulk.

She can do this. She can say it. One way or another, even if it needs to be clumsy as hell, she can stop hiding and put into words the wild and overwhelming feeling in her own chest.

Finally, with her heart racing and her chest gone tight, she opens her mouth and asks, "You ever consider falling in love with your best friend?"

Jackie falls silent, but she doesn't pull away.

And Lou reminds herself to breathe.

An Intimate Morning

Charlie is still squinting when he shambles into the kitchen, bleary and sleep-deprived and desperate for the coffee he can already smell percolating on the counter. But when he gets close enough to actually see the coffee machine, through the glare of too much daylight pouring through the bright and tidy kitchen, he finds there's not enough liquid to fill even half a mug. Sal must've put the pot on only a few minutes ago.

God damn it.

It's Charlie's own fault he's so exhausted this morning. At least, it's mostly Charlie's fault. The part where Sal kept him up half the night with distracting and intimate activities? That was a team effort. But afterwards, when Charlie forced himself to stay awake reading a long assignment for this morning's lecture? That was all him, and probably a waste of energy. He can't remember a single thing from the chapters he lurched through last night. He sure hopes he took notes in the margins and highlighted relevant topics, so at least he'll be able to fake it if the professor calls on him.

He's staring forlornly down at the slowly dripping coffee maker when a wall of heat closes in along his back. The sensations of broad muscle and bare skin make Charlie glad he didn't bother putting on a shirt. He shivers as powerful arms wrap around him in a fond embrace.

"You look like hell," Sal murmurs, wry humor softening the words. He leans forward, propping his chin on Charlie's shoulder and nuzzling the side of his neck.

"Mmm." Charlie melts into his boyfriend's arms and lets himself be held, trusting Sal to keep him from falling, even as Charlie's eyes drift shut in a dizzy tangle of exhaustion and contentment.

"Anything I can do to help?"

"Make the coffee brew faster?" Charlie suggests without opening his eyes.

"I'd love to." Sal presses a kiss to the crook of his shoulder, and the rough texture of stubble tickles Charlie's skin. "But that's not a superpower I possess. Got a second choice?"

Charlie turns his head, pleading without words for a lazy kiss. Sal indulges him without hesitation, arms tightening around Charlie, mouth hot and demanding. It's an awkward angle, but they make it work, and Charlie shivers at the way Sal crowds him forward even more firmly against the counter.

God, Charlie loves this. For all that it's only been a few weeks since he and Sal started fucking around—and a couple days at most since they made their understanding more official—it's amazing how easy this feels. How comfortable he finds himself in Sal's space. How quickly his arousal begins to coil and warm in his belly, despite the weight of fatigue dragging him towards the floor.

The adrenaline of desire isn't quite as instant or Pavlovian as coffee, but it's *good*, and Charlie drags in a shallow breath. His ass still aches from how enthusiastically Sal fucked him last night. He's not up for a repeat performance of that particular activity yet, but the longing to be touched is powerful just the same, and there are other ways Sal can give him what he needs.

Without breaking from the kiss, Charlie covers one of Sal's hands with his own and guides the touch lower. Down from his waist. Down the front of his boxers. Down to the stiffening line of Charlie's cock, where he is suddenly desperate to be touched.

Sal hums an approving sound and curls a decisive grip around Charlie's length. A firm, dry stroke along the shaft—just shy of uncomfortable, and gloriously good—is all it takes for Charlie to go from burgeoning interest to rigid erection. He huffs a frantic little moan, his hips jolting forward. Sal only chuckles and swipes his thumb through the precome gathering at the tip of Charlie's cock, then drags his fist along the entire length once more.

Charlie blinks his eyes open and stares down, fascinated as always at the sight of Sal's hand moving beneath his boxers. The fabric bunches and stretches in an obscene rhythm over the increasingly intense touch, and Charlie's breath comes faster while he watches. He adores the way Sal touches him. Already pleasure is mounting hot and wild beneath his skin. His belly feels tight with need, and he whimpers at the way Sal grips suddenly harder.

"Can you keep quiet when I finish you off?" Sal's question rumbles in Charlie's ear, sending a shiver along his spine.

"I... I don't know," Charlie admits. The answer is probably yes. He mostly trusts himself to exercise a modicum of self-restraint and not wake Sal's neighbors at this completely ungodly hour. But he also can't deny the scrap of doubt lingering inside him. And beyond that, the knowledge of *how* Sal will probably help if Charlie asks, which is enticing all on its own.

"Do you need my help?" Sal's hand is moving faster now, stroking with an urgent intensity that is making it very difficult for Charlie to think.

"*Yes*," Charlie gasps, shuddering in Sal's arms, chasing his pleasure with clumsy and ineffective movements. "Please, yes, help me."

A heartbeat later, Sal's free arm unwinds from around his waist, and that big hand moves to cover Charlie's mouth. Heavy and somehow simultaneously protective and possessive. Charlie lets his eyes drift shut, an ecstasy of sensation flooding through him. He feels so incongruously safe like this, held against his boyfriend's chest, trapped against the counter, cherished and giddy and out of control. Sal's answering erection grinds forward against his backside, and Charlie savors the frantic notion that he is not the only one on the verge of falling apart.

He loses himself in the rough slide of the hand along his cock, the heat of the mouth nipping at his throat, the shared sense of urgency pulsing between them like a moment out of time.

"Come for me, love," Sal growls, the words a gruff and inescapable command.

With a cry muffled beneath Sal's enormous hand, Charlie obeys.

Something Green

Lane doesn't expect to come home to an empty house.

Jordan is usually back from work by the time he arrives, but today his partner is nowhere to be seen. Even their truck is missing from its usual place, out front by the curb. The neighbors have avoided the space in deference to its usual occupant, but the empty spot is an unexpected sight.

Lane doesn't worry, for all that this break from routine jars him. Jordan can do whatever the hell they want with their afternoon. They've got no obligation to check in with Lane in the absence of specific plans.

But Lane's confusion amplifies when he reaches the front door and finds it unlocked. He can perfectly well believe Jordan going out without consulting him, rarely though it happens, but he can't imagine them leaving the house unlocked and driving away. Jordan is far too meticulous for such mistakes.

"Babe?" he calls now, as he steps inside and nudges the door shut with his hip. No response as he unslings the satchel from his shoulder and sets it beside the stairs, mindful of his laptop. "Jordan? You home?"

Still nothing, and he moves deeper into the house. A little worried now, if he's honest. The open lock and silence sneak beneath his skin and let slip a shiver of apprehension. The living room is empty too. The kitchen. The laundry room and back hall. He's about to reroute and make his way upstairs when he hears—as though from far away—a string of emphatic cursing.

Not far away, he realizes after a heartbeat of delay. *Outside*. Lane moves farther into the hallway that leads to the backyard, and when he approaches the door, he spots movement through the small panes of glass. The knob turns beneath his hand—also unlocked—and as the door swings open, relief floods through Lane so sharply he feels silly for worrying in the first place.

Jordan works busily in the backyard—in the overgrown garden plot that neither one of them has ever touched—brandishing an enormous pair of garden shears. The truck has been backed close, right at the edge of the rutted alley, the gate lowered to allow for easier loading of a small mountain of dead plant matter. Jordan's back is to the house, their broad shoulders bunching and flexing with exertion. As far as Lane can tell, they're doing battle with the desiccated remnants of some vining, creeping bramble.

And it is *not* going well.

Another string of frustrated expletives erupts, and Lane grins as he considers what the neighbors must be making of this spectacle. Jordan seems to be struggling now with an especially fiendish vine. After a moment, the repetitive stream of cursing cuts off with a delighted and victorious, "*Ha*!"

Lane waits until they lower the shears—no call for causing surprise when a sharp implement is in play—before calling out. "What on earth are you doing?"

Jordan doesn't appear to startle at the question, but they turn quickly, meeting Lane's eyes with a smile that can only be described as impish. The glint of excitement renders their dark face—always handsome and sweet—into something so radiant that for several seconds Lane can't breathe.

Air returns to his lungs soon enough. And maybe it's ridiculous to still be so thoroughly smitten by his partner after nearly five years, but Jordan is stunning to behold. Lane would defy *anyone* to be unmoved by this view.

Jordan sets the shears down on an old wooden bench, eyes sparkling with warmth. Their sturdy frame is distractingly highlighted by the spring sun. A sweat-slick t-shirt clings to every line of their torso, familiar muscle and round softness, and Lane's pulse speeds. God, Jordan is so *big*—a whole lot bigger than his own skinny five-foot frame—and Lane never tires of looking at them.

"I'm clearing the garden plot," Jordan explains. Lane gives in to the urge to approach. Flecks of dirt have smeared along Jordan's powerful arms, and Lane's glad to see heavy gardening gloves protecting their hands.

"Yes," Lane says agreeably, "but *why*?"

"Because I want to start a garden. Something green and outdoors."

Lane is nearly within reach now. "I've known you almost a decade, and you have never once expressed an interest in gardening." He would remember. He hoards and memorizes every detail about Jordan, forever greedy for each new scrap of information that manages to catch him off guard.

Jordan gives a shrug and tugs off the gloves, tossing them down beside the shears. The faint hint of sheepishness does nothing to dampen the glitter of excitement in their lovely brown eyes. "I want to try something new this year."

And now, *now* Lane is close enough to touch. He has to grip the front of Jordan's t-shirt to tug them down for a kiss—even on tiptoes he can't quite reach Jordan's mouth without a team effort—and is disappointed when Jordan eases back after only a couple seconds.

"Hey," he protests, not letting go.

The corners of Jordan's eyes scrunch with amusement. "I'm a mess, Lane."

Yes. They are. It's glorious. Lane wants to be a mess too.

He grins a wide, wicked smile. "So get me dirty already," he says and tugs Jordan down again.

This time Jordan stays. Wraps strong arms around him, and then—once Lane's arms are clasped securely around their shoulders in answer—hoists him up. Lane wraps his legs around Jordan's thick waist, steadying himself as the kiss deepens.

He does not feel nearly as filthy as he craves by the time they break for air. But Jordan doesn't put him down, and Lane does not let go. If both of them are breathing hard, that's just a sign of more good things to come.

"So," Lane murmurs, despite the strain of arousal making his voice rumble. "What are you going to grow?"

Jordan laughs instead of answering—loud and strong—and carries him inside.

Smitten

CJ doesn't believe in love at first sight.

The very idea feels naive and unrealistic. She's not some teenager, to get carried away by a rush of butterflies at the sight of a pretty face.

But she also can't deny the instant and unrelenting hold Erika Chance has taken on her heart—not to mention on other, significantly less sentimental parts of her anatomy. A week since first catching sight of the burly mechanic, CJ is still reeling.

Now she needs to walk back into Chance Auto Repair to pick up her car, and her pulse starts racing before she's even finished paying the cab fare. How is she supposed to do this? How can she go in casual and pay her bill like it's no big deal, when her heart is already firing off at ninety miles an hour?

A deep breath does little to calm her. But CJ strides forward anyway, through the first open bay door and out of the bright glare of sunlight, into the enormous garage.

Her eyes find Erika immediately, because no matter how firmly she's admonished herself to play it cool, her senses remain on high alert. Erika stands at the far side of the wide cement floor, working on the front end of a massive truck. Her whole upper body is bent forward, folded down beneath the propped hood. At this distance, CJ can't tell what Erika is working on, only that it must be something heavy.

CJ's arrival has gone unnoticed, but then, of course it has. Even without the physical distance separating them across the garage floor, why should Erika notice her arrival? The woman clearly has her hands full with more important matters.

It takes CJ several reluctant moments to turn away from the sight of powerful shoulders and strong arms straining at their task. Then another handful of seconds before she convinces her legs to walk toward the office at the back of the garage.

The office stands empty. A wide wall of windows makes it easy to tell there's no one inside, even before CJ draws close, and she pauses at the open doorframe.

Vivid memory rises, sudden but not unexpected. CJ's first visit to the garage just over a week ago—her first glimpse of Erika in this very office. The impression was powerful and instantaneous: a stern face, deep alto voice, and a handshake that was strong but not crushing. Erika is a gorgeous mountain of a woman, and CJ could've stared at those wide shoulders and piercing eyes all day. Instead, she did her best to pay attention while Erika explained paperwork and fees. She absorbed almost none of the information, despite being absolutely riveted.

Now, faced with an empty office, CJ's mind begins to wander. She's always possessed an active imagination, and it's no surprise to find herself fantasizing about Erika. About strong hands holding her down, holding her close, holding her still. A silky voice murmuring in her ear, offering up intimacies and orders. A generous mouth trailing kisses down her skin, tasting and claiming every inch of her. A broad chest pressing directly along CJ's back, weight bearing her down, pinning her in place over the hastily cleared desk.

Fucking hell. CJ's blood is heating fast, and she does her best to cut her imaginings short. This is neither the time nor the place for such thoughts.

"Hey," comes a rumbled greeting, and CJ turns to find Erika standing just behind her.

"Hi." She steps aside to let Erika through the office door, then follows a pace behind. Her face burns hot, not from embarrassment, but from want. Her own stride makes her urgently aware of the warmth that has settled low in her belly. "I'm here to pick up my car."

She doesn't sound the least bit suave. Mostly she sounds like she's been caught sneaking around somewhere she doesn't belong, breathless and a little shaky. But at least she's still forming coherent sentences.

"Got your invoice ready." Erika grabs a stapled set of papers off the desk and hands them over, a sweet smile softening her features. She obviously expects CJ to flip through the papers and check for errors, but CJ just reaches into her back pocket for the check she wrote before calling a cab. This morning's voicemail gave her the dollar amount, and she's confident the garage's paperwork is in order. She wouldn't have come so far out of her way in the first place if Chance Auto hadn't come highly recommended.

"Thanks." Erika accepts the check. Then, like an afterthought, she pulls a brown envelope out of the top desk drawer. "Here."

Erika tilts the envelope to slide a car key into CJ's hand.

"She's parked in the side lot," Erika says. "Oh, and you'll need some brake work done in a couple months. Let me know if you want a quote."

"Sure. I'll be in touch." CJ will definitely call for that quote. She looks forward to having an excuse—any excuse—to come back, even if Chance Auto is a significant distance from her usual orbit.

When Erika shakes her hand a moment later, the strength in her grip sends a visceral pulse of desire along CJ's already flushed skin. She can't help the pleased smile that stretches across her face in answer to all the wordless potential in Erika's touch. The subtle act of lingering just a little too long that, judging by the unconcerned expression on the woman's face, Erika isn't consciously aware of doing.

Yes, CJ will be back in a couple months. Sooner, if she can conjure a believable reason without sabotaging her car outright.

Something tells her she'll be spending a lot of time in this garage.

A Kiss to Start

The problem with falling in love with your best friend is that eventually—inevitably—it becomes impossible to keep your mouth shut. Connor has been fighting a losing battle for months, but sometimes it feels like eons. The secret has been bursting to get out of him, ever since the moment he put two and two together and came up with a number significantly greater than four.

Connor isn't a good liar, at least not when it comes to selling a story for the long haul. His dark eyes have always been too expressive for his own good, and his big heart doesn't help matters. He knew from the start that he would never be able to keep this squashed down where it belongs, in the secret recesses of his soul where it can't complicate the most important relationship in his life.

Honestly, he lasted longer than he expected to in the end—though the feat probably had more to do with Tim spending a semester abroad than any better sense or discretion on Connor's part. It's easier to guard a secret when interactions are limited to emails and text messages across wildly incompatible time zones.

But eventually Christmas break reaches across the distance, bringing Tim with it. Suddenly he's a constant presence, unavoidable and underfoot as they both fall into familiar routines. Tim's stocky frame fills Connor's tiny apartment like this is the one place he truly belongs, welcome and yet utterly maddening. Connor covets his company and yet having Tim so close frays his dwindling equilibrium, little by endless little.

Even worse, he's finding it harder and harder to let Tim leave. Every time Tim stands up from Connor's lumpy couch—every time he stretches his shoulders and starts searching for his leather jacket to head home—it's all Connor can do not to plead with him to stay, just a little longer.

The night Connor kisses Tim, he barely gets a taste before backpedaling and apologizing, falling off his own couch as he scrambles away. Mortification flushes his cheeks with feverish heat, and his tailbone aches from landing on the hardwood floor. God, he didn't even ask for permission. The silence had been so inviting, strange and intimate and different from their usual easy closeness, but that didn't give him the right to assume.

When Connor finally raises his eyes, he finds Tim staring at him. Tim's eyes are wide, expression tinged with disbelief and—

Is that a smile?

"You just kissed me." Tim's voice dips low, deeper than usual.

"No I didn't." It's an absurd denial. Connor rises unsteadily to his feet, unable to take his eyes off of Tim. He doesn't understand why Tim's smile seems to be growing wider.

"You did. You definitely kissed me."

"Um," Connor says. He needs to retreat and regroup, but he stands there instead, gawping helplessly. His brain has caught and stuck somewhere between *oh god* and *what now?*

"For fuck's sake." Tim rolls his eyes and breathes an exasperated laugh. He reaches for Connor, grabbing him by the belt loops and yanking him down. Connor lands astride Tim's lap, which puts them almost exactly eye-to-eye. An electric instant snags between them and stretches taut. The television—still replaying the menu screen for their abandoned video game—pings cheerfully.

Connor can't breathe.

"You are completely impossible," Tim says.

Then he kisses Connor soundly on the mouth.

Things get a little hectic after that, not that Connor has any desire to complain. There's more kissing—quite a lot of kissing, actually— and then Connor finds a spot beneath Tim's jaw that makes his friend moan and arch against him. Delicious decadence. Connor hasn't felt this clumsy about physical touch in ages, but Tim doesn't seem to mind. Somehow, with concerted effort between the two of them, they manage to work belts and flies open, drag t-shirts off, get their hands on bare skin.

Connor shivers, giddy and overwhelmed. From the panting, gasping rumble of Tim's voice in his ear, he clearly isn't the only one.

They goad each other quickly to the precipice, and then right over the edge without hesitation or restraint.

"Christ, Connor," Tim mutters in the overheated quiet that follows. "Why didn't you say something sooner?" They're curled more lazily together now, Tim all hard edges and Connor soft and pliant and tucked close in his arms—an intertwined tangle of sated limbs, their bodies stretched lengthwise along the couch. Connor's shirt has been sacrificed to the cause of wiping themselves clean, but it's a small price to pay for not needing to move.

"What? Like you did?" Connor retorts. "Wait, that's right, you were just as chicken-shit as me."

"Rude." Tim's breath ruffles Connor's hair and tickles the side of his neck. His voice purrs with fondness and something deeper— something that might be new, or might have been there for ages, with Connor too willfully oblivious to hear it. Whatever the emotion, it resonates in Connor's chest, a perfect match for things he doubts he will ever have words to express.

Warmth spreads through him, and Connor huffs a delighted laugh. A softer hum. Then he tucks his head beneath Tim's jaw and lets contentment roll through him as his eyes drift tiredly shut.

A Terrible Idea

"This is the worst idea you've ever had," Elsie protests, though her broad shoulders are shaking with laughter as she kicks the study room door shut behind her. "We're going to get caught, and the head librarian is going to yell at us, and then I don't know what will happen after that, but I'm sure it will be mortifying."

Kat studies her girlfriend with an appreciative gaze, taking in the cozy sweater concealing powerful arms, the sly glint in umber eyes, the flush of warmth across her skin. A flicker of amusement cuts through Elsie's completely unconvincing effort to look stern.

"We won't get caught," Kat insists, stepping closer without touching. She stands near enough to feel Elsie's body heat along her front—near enough she needs to tip her head back to meet the ever-present affection in Elsie's expressive eyes.

Kat tried teaching Elsie to play poker once upon a time. It was a hopeless experiment in the end, as Elsie's eyes always give everything away. The woman is too earnest, and too honest, and Kat adores her for it. She lets her own wild adoration shine in her face, and grins when Elsie sways toward her.

"You're sure?" Elsie sounds hopeful now. A spark of desire kindles in her eyes.

"The day before a holiday? No one is even using the library tonight. And the head librarian owes me at least six favors. We don't need to worry about her." Which won't even matter if they never get caught in the first place—fooling around in this stuffy little study room with no windows—but Elsie has always been the sort to appreciate contingency plans, and Kat will always be happy to humor her.

"Okay," says Elsie, and then moves so quickly Kat's head spins.

Oh, it's not just her head, Kat realizes with a shiver of delight. It's the room itself spinning— or at least Kat spinning within it—as Elsie reverses their positions and pushes her roughly back against the door. The kiss that follows is bright and intense, and Kat melts as Elsie pins her even harder, leaning down to meet her.

Elsie hasn't always been comfortable doing this—bringing all her strength to bear and pushing Kat around. She's too much of a teddy bear, too sweet and thoughtful, and it wasn't until Kat enthusiastically suggested the experiment that Elsie got onboard with this sort of rougher handling.

Now they are both reaping the rewards, and Kat's belly tightens with growing arousal as Elsie kisses and kisses and kisses her. By the time powerful hands drag and shove her again, pressing her face-first against the cool woodgrain, Kat's lips are tingling and she can't stop rubbing her thighs together. She is achingly aroused, desperate to be touched, and she breathes a low moan when Elsie shoves in close along her back and hikes Kat's skirt impatiently up her thighs.

It's a short skirt, and tight enough that it catches at her hips and stays out of the way. Elsie slips a deft hand between her legs and drags a hot press of fingertips over Kat's panties, rubbing the fabric between her folds. The thin cotton is already damp with Kat's need, and it grows even more wet as she grinds eagerly down on Elsie's hand, saturating the fabric. She might be begging already. She might be moaning a messy amalgam of *please* and *yes* and *more*. But she isn't sure, too focused on the pleasure building at her core, the urgent stroking pressure of Elsie's fingers exploring and teasing.

She cries out when the pad of Elsie's thumb circles her clit, and then Elsie's free hand is over her mouth to quiet her.

"We'll definitely get caught if you do that," Elsie husks. But she doesn't sound angry. She sounds turned-on and possessive, and she doesn't stop touching Kat as she breathes the admonishment into feverish skin.

A moment later, Elsie's touch disappears— but Kat has only long enough to whimper her protest before Elsie's hand slips beneath her panties. And oh, if the friction through soft cotton was maddening, the sensation of skin against skin is enough to make Kat wail. Thank fuck for the big hand still squashing the bottom half of her face. She rides down harder on Elsie's fingers as they part her slick folds, trace overheated skin, rub mercilessly at her clit. The pleasure is so sharp and intense that Kat's whole body stretches taut, overwhelming her, making her shudder.

Then Elsie's long fingers thrust directly inside her. Two at first. A blunt and welcome rhythm. A third when she's sure Kat can take it.

When Elsie grinds the heel of her palm simultaneously against Kat's clit, it's enough. It's too much. It's a bright supernova of sensation, a live wire making contact with her core, a crest of orgasm so powerful that it's a damn good thing Elsie's palm is there to muffle her cry. Kat has never been quiet when she comes, and under normal circumstances, she knows Elsie would rather hear her keen.

Kat has no room in her head for caution right now, as she rides up and up, into the stratosphere. Elsie's fingers fuck her relentlessly, continuing until they force a second even more shattering orgasm out of her.

"Oh," Kat breathes, when at last she *can* breathe again. Elsie still holds her against the door. Elsie's hand is still between her legs, Elsie's long fingers a firm presence inside her, impossible to ignore.

"You alright?" Elsie nuzzles at the line of her throat, kissing her still racing pulse point.

"Yeah."

"Good," Elsie purrs.

Then those fingers resume their thrusting, and the world shatters to pieces once more.

The Easiest Thing

Anxiety sucks.

Jake sits amid a mountain of pillows, curling himself up as small as he can get on the wide-cushioned bench of the window seat. It's his favorite spot in the entire house—a cozy little alcove that's usually bright and sunny through the panes of glass—but tonight it's all storm and rain.

The rain might be soothing if he weren't so twisted up in his own head. Everything seems uglier, messier, more difficult when his brain plays this particular set of tricks on him. Even now, his rational mind fights valiantly to remind him there are any number of perfectly benign reasons his best friends aren't answering his text messages. Neither Laura nor Sasha has ever been the type of person to mess with his head on purpose. They know how Jake gets.

If they're upset about something, they *tell him*. Radio silence doesn't mean anything beyond the apparent fact that they're both busy.

But knowing these things with his brain does nothing to stop Jake's heart from catastrophizing. And until at least one of them sends a reply, Jake is going to be caught in the dodgy landscape of his own head, replaying every conversation he's ever had with them that might have gone awry.

The room around him has gotten darker as the storm outside rolls across the sky, which means only the slant of light from the hallway touches the grim shadows closing in from all sides.

He startles at the sound of footsteps climbing the staircase, and realizes Casey must've gotten home while Jake was spiraling. He didn't hear the garage door announcing his roommate's return. But then, he never hears much of anything when he's really falling apart.

"Jake?" Casey calls from the end of the hallway, and the sound of his voice sends a bloom of yearning gratitude through Jake's chest.

"In the library," he calls, and his voice sounds faint and pathetic next to Casey's rumbling baritone.

"Why are the lights off?" Casey appears in the door, bulky silhouette making Jake feel steadier than he has all day.

A moment later, Casey turns on the standing lamp in the corner, and the stained-glass contours of the lampshade cast a patchwork rainbow over his perplexed expression. His jaw bears the inevitable stubble that always grows back by mid-afternoon, no matter how closely he shaves, and his eyes are narrowed with worry.

Jake watches and doesn't answer. His voice has gone too tight in his throat. When Casey actually *looks* at him, the confused expression melts away in favor of softer understanding.

"Bad day?" Casey murmurs, approaching slowly.

"Yeah," Jake manages to rasp past the clog of irrational emotion in his throat.

Casey collects the old blue quilt off the recliner on his way across the room. "Scoot over."

A grateful shiver rushes beneath Jake's skin as he adjusts to make room. There isn't really space for two grown men in the little alcove, but Casey folds his big frame down anyway, sitting against the wall and tugging Jake tight to his side. It's the easiest thing in the world to melt into the protective circle of Casey's arms, and Jake presses closer with a sigh. His head rests over Casey's heart, and he listens to the reassuring rhythm as he matches his breathing to the rise and fall of Casey's chest. In. Out. In. Out.

Casey smells like rain.

Gentle fingers brush a chaotic fluff of hair behind Jake's ear, and he spares a single unrealistic moment wondering if Casey will kiss him.

They've dated in the past. They'll probably date again someday—at least, if Jake has any say in the matter—but at the moment they are friends. Roommates. Something like family, and something else entirely, and Jake knows better than to push.

He's not going to be greedy, when he's already got something so good right here.

"Better?" Casey murmurs.

"Yeah." Jake snuggles deeper, practically crawling into Casey's lap. He wishes he could disappear like this, skinny frame folded into the warm and perfect safety of Casey's arms. Nothing can touch him here. His anxieties remain, a relentless hum of tension behind his ribs, but the sensation doesn't feel nearly as much like panic while Casey is holding him. He'll have to face the anxiety eventually, but in this moment, nothing can hurt him.

"Sorry," Jake whispers. "Bad brain stuff."

Casey breathes a comprehending hum. "Anything I can do to help?"

"Yes," Jake says. Then, before Casey can ask what, he adds, "This."

Casey's answering chuckle is low and fond, and he presses a kiss to the crown of Jake's head. "Yeah. Okay."

Simple Equations

If it weren't for the lit window Dana glimpsed when they drove up to the building, they might assume they're walking into an empty apartment. There are no lights on in the kitchen or the living room. Not even the weak bulb in the hallway has been turned on in deference to a sunset long past, which guarantees Ashley hasn't stood up from her desk in at least three hours.

Dana huffs an exasperated, nearly soundless laugh as they step inside and lock the front door, then kick their shoes off into the tiny corner that functions as a mudroom. Their messenger bag lands with a thump on the kitchen table as they pass by, then head down the short hall leading deeper into the apartment they share with their girlfriend.

Finally, drawing near the study, Dana catches a glimmer of illumination. Under the closed door, a bright sliver confirms what they saw from outside: Ashley is home, and awake, and probably buried so deep in her logarithmic equations that she has no idea what time it is.

To be fair, the hour isn't actually that late. But it's definitely past supper time—Dana has come home famished—and they're pretty confident Ashley hasn't surfaced from her work long enough to eat.

Dana doesn't particularly want to startle her, so they tap their knuckles against the smooth woodgrain of the door, in case their footsteps along the dark hallway weren't loud enough to signal their presence. The knocking gets no response, so they try a little louder. It's not that they aren't entitled to barge into this shared office whenever they please—but they also know just how focused Ashley can get. It's a trait Dana finds both exasperating and adorable, and they aren't especially surprised in this moment.

When a third, even more forceful attempt still has no effect, Dana finally gives up and opens the door. The brightness on the other side makes them squint for several seconds, while their eyes grudgingly adjust from shadowy hallway to bright study.

Once they can see anything at all beyond broad, basic shapes, the first thing their eyes find is Ashley. Always Ashley. Sitting at the desk in the corner, her dark curls askew in the particular way that means agitation has her running fingers repeatedly through her hair. The problem sets have clearly been uncooperative tonight. No wonder she's so far gone. Her warm brown profile scrunches in a complicated amalgam of frustration and focus, and her expressive mouth twists unmistakably down at the corner.

Ashley does not look like she's having a good time, and Dana's heart gives a protective twinge at the sight.

"Maybe you should take a break, Ash," Dana says, but they're not surprised the admonition fails to break through the fog. It will take something more tactile to do the trick, and Dana steps farther into the room. Their own reflection moves in the window, broad shoulders and severely short hair, as they approach the desk and set a hand on the back of Ashley's chair.

Ashley doesn't look up or even seem to notice Dana in her peripheral vision. If anything, she's glaring even harder at the equations scribbled across her notebooks, as though the numbers she usually trusts have betrayed her. The expression has no business being so goddamn cute.

"Hey," Dana says softly, and this time they set a hand to Ashley's nape.

Ashley doesn't startle the way Dana expects. Instead, she melts beneath the touch, breathing a low sigh as her eyes flicker shut. Dana's fingers curl more closely around the back of her neck, and the last of the tension drains from Ashley's shoulders and face.

"You okay?" Dana asks, digging their fingers in a little—exerting pressure right where Ashley's muscles always get tight when she studies. "How long have you been at this?"

"Not long." Ashley doesn't say the words like a lie—she clearly believes them—but then she follows them up by adding, "Since two, maybe? I've only got a few more problems left."

"Ash." Dana huffs, and doesn't bother trying to rein in the amused incredulity in their voice.

"It's past seven. Please tell me you remembered to eat lunch before you buried yourself in here."

"I... think I ate lunch," Ashley says, but the way her pitch drifts higher at the end is not reassuring.

"*Ashley.*"

"I really need to finish this assignment," Ashley protests, but her tone—sheepish and a little plaintive—says she knows she fucked up. Ashley is smart. Unreasonably smart in so many ways, but also forgetful and distracted when it comes to things like this. She knows damn well she needs to take better care of herself, if she wants her brain running at peak capacity. And Dana knows how frustrating Ashley finds being coddled. It makes for a complicated balance.

"You need food." Dana tugs at the chair, and Ashley lets herself be coaxed to her feet. "You want burgers or spaghetti?" Dana's pretty sure they have fixings on hand for both, but there are also plenty of nearby places that deliver.

"Burgers," Ashley says, and the decisiveness is reassuring. It means she hasn't crossed over the dubious line into so-hungry-nothing-sounds-good territory. "Definitely burgers. Do we have any of that fancy aioli left?"

"No idea," Dana admits. "Hey. C'mere."

Dana intercepts before Ashley can build any actual momentum toward the office door, catching her by the arm and tugging her closer. Ashley sways easily into their space, offering Dana a tired but earnest smile that softens Ashley's whole expression. When Ashley's arms slip around their waist, Dana answers without a word, by curling their fingers along Ashley's jaw and drawing her into a kiss.

As kisses go, it's quick. Getting some food into their girlfriend is still Dana's top priority. But they linger anyway, savoring the moment and holding Ashley close.

On the Edge

For a time, sitting back on his heels to take in the view laid out so beautifully before him, the only sounds Michael hears are rain on the window and Jay's panting breath. A smile touches his face as he studies Jay's naked body, artfully splayed across Michael's bed. Wiry muscle and smooth skin make for a lovely tableau atop the maroon comforter.

Jay lies trembling on his back—a whirlwind of unsated arousal—trapped and helpless, calming by grudging degrees.

Michael reads pleading hunger in Jay's squirming energy. Such an obvious need to be touched, and Michael will oblige only once he's confident the urgency has receded. He has already strung Jay along for nearly an hour. There's an art to keeping a needy man on edge without letting him come.

Keeping perfectly still is a cruel tactic on Michael's part, especially when the blindfold across Jay's eyes makes it impossible for him to glean any information from the stillness.

A bit of simple but delicate rope work makes it equally impossible for Jay to sate his own needs. He is utterly at Michael's mercy, which is exactly how Michael loves to keep him. Even without being able to see Jay's wrists, tied and pinned beneath his back as they are, it's obvious he is straining within his bonds. Fighting a losing battle. There's nothing he can do to rush Michael's calculated game.

"Are you quite finished?" Michael teases, when at last Jay subsides.

"Fuck you." The words, gasped and shaking, carry no anger—only desperate pleading.

"Do you want an orgasm or not?"

The question freezes Jay in place, and Michael smiles wider at the startled show of restraint. Jay's face is flushed, his nipples reddened and stiff from the attentions of Michael's fingers and teeth, his cock hard and curving deliciously toward his belly.

"You're just messing with me." Jay's words rumble low and gruff. He sounds fucked-out from such a prolonged denial of the satisfaction he craves. Of course his voice is gone to gravel; Michael has kept him sobbing and screaming for an eon. He has worked Jay open with gentle fingers. He's covered him with kisses and pinned him to the bed. Michael has already fucked him, because there is a time and a place for selfishness. He thoroughly enjoyed taking his own pleasure while continuing to deny Jay any release.

"You think I'd tease you like that?" Michael murmurs, pure silk.

Jay trembles in place. "Yes."

"You wound me."

Jay snorts, and the sound is wry despite his riled state. "Bullshit. You'll just... Fuck... You'll just work me up again, and you still won't let me come, and I hate you so fucking much, oh god, please touch me!"

"Ask nicely," Michael chides. He does not bother pointing out that Jay could end this in a heartbeat, simply by using his safe word.

They both know Jay is nowhere near offering that particular surrender.

Jay's answering whimper is perfect agony, but after a moment he breathes a softer, more deferential, "Please touch me, sir."

"Mmm." Michael tugs Jay's legs wide so that he can position himself between them. He relishes Jay's sharp inhale, and the inevitable tensing of anticipation. This marvelous and expressive man is by far the most responsive companion Michael has ever invited into his bed.

"*Please*," Jay moans as Michael leans down and exhales, hot and teasing, over Jay's straining cock. His hips try to thrust, but Michael sets a hand to Jay's stomach and holds him down. He will do this at his own pace, and Jay will both adore and curse him for it.

Perhaps this time, Michael really will allow him to come.

More pleading follows, shaky and shrill, and Michael drops his jaw and takes in the waiting length. Jay gasps and falls silent, trying again to arch off the bed—again thwarted by Michael's strength—and groans breathless curses that twine through the otherwise quiet bedroom. Rain pummels the window harder now, but

Michael barely hears the patter beneath Jay's filthy litany.

He ducks his head to take more, suppressing his gag reflex as the blunt tip nudges the back of his throat. He doesn't try to swallow Jay down—he's never possessed that particular skill—but he seals his lips tight around the shaft and hollows his cheeks with suction. Possessive pleasure zings through him as a shattered whimper interrupts Jay's string of expletives.

Michael bobs his head back up and drags the flat of his tongue across the tip of Jay's cock, then teases at the slit. Jay's breath hitches audibly, and Michael gives his tongue an answering swirl.

"Oh, fuck, sir!" Jay bucks beneath his hold. "Fuck, *please*!"

Michael would laugh, fond and delighted, if his mouth weren't full. Such demanding disobedience. Instead he ducks low, sucking hard, only to retreat a moment later and allow Jay's entire impatient length to slide from his mouth.

"What a shame," he purrs, giving Jay's cock an idle stroke with his free hand. "You were doing so well."

"Sir?" Jay sounds like he is trying very hard to remain calm and coherent, and failing utterly.

"You know better than to backseat drive." Michael tightens his grip around Jay's length, then ducks his head to place a teasing kiss at the very tip. "It's a pity."

"Sir, please!" Jay rasps as Michael begins to stroke the same hand up and down, firm and steady and utterly without remorse. The frenzy in Jay's voice makes it clear he knows he has just postponed his satisfaction again, and that there's no telling how much longer Michael intends to torture him with this endless avalanche of gentleness.

"No," Michael proclaims cheerfully, speeding his caresses, paying close attention so that he will be ready to let go before Jay can reach climax. "Relax, my dear. Just lie back and let me take care of you."

Jay's answering sob is music to his ears.

In the Library

"Oh, for fuck's sake," Nyla mutters, unable to keep the fondness and humor out of her voice as Colby's hands curl around her shoulders and shove. "The library is for studying, not canoodling."

"Then they should've chosen less versatile chairs." Colby's retort is accompanied by her most impish grin, and by her sudden weight straddling Nyla's thighs. And really, the woman makes an excellent point. If whoever designed the university library didn't want students engaging in these sorts of shenanigans, they really should've filled the place with less accommodating chairs. These big, blocky seats aren't especially comfortable for long study sessions—but they're wide and sturdy, more than up to the task of holding Nyla's muscular bulk and Colby's gangly frame simultaneously.

Still, Nyla tries to look stern as she peers into Colby's face. She takes in the mischievous flash of teeth, the messy mop of hair, the dimple creasing one cheek. Colby looks charmingly at ease, the perfect counterpoint to Nyla's own buttoned-up and habitually grouchy appearance.

Nyla is not *actually* grouchy. Her face just occasionally needs to be reminded that smiling is a perfectly acceptable way to respond to positive emotions.

"Oh, stop it," Colby teases, ready as always to nudge Nyla into distraction. "It's ten o'clock at night. The only people here are panicking about exams, and none of them will stand up from their study carrels before closing time. Plus the two temps manning the circulation desk downstairs, who definitely won't be re-shelving anything tonight. No one's going to wander through at this hour, and the library doesn't close until eleven. We won't get caught *canoodling*."

Colby echoes the word with such cheeky cheerfulness that Nyla snorts and shakes her head—exasperated and fond in equal measure, as she always finds herself where her ridiculous girlfriend is concerned.

"You're a terrible influence," Nyla informs Colby blandly.

"You love me for it." Colby slides her hands smoothly, slowly up the sides of Nyla's neck, framing Nyla's jaw between her palms as she bumps their foreheads together.

"I love you for many reasons." Nyla stops exercising her apparently unnecessary self-restraint, reaching past Colby to cap and set aside her highlighter, and then looping both arms loosely around Colby's waist. "I'm not sure that's one of them, honestly."

"Oh, it definitely is." Colby's grin spreads so wide she looks a little feral, and then she's ducking forward, pressing a light kiss to the corner of Nyla's mouth. "Trust me. I'm a scientist. I possess keen powers of analysis and observation."

"You're biased and you know it." But Nyla doesn't care about this argument anymore, and she tilts the angle of her head just slightly, just enough to catch Colby's mouth with her own. Colby tastes sweet—like maybe she's just finished a can of soda in her own half-assed attempt to stay awake and get some studying done—and her fingers thread eagerly into Nyla's hair, as the kiss deepens into something suggestive and filthy.

"See?" Nyla gasps, when Colby finally draws back, leaving them both breathing hard. "Terrible influence."

"Yes. Well." Colby nuzzles beneath Nyla's jaw, squirming on her lap in a way that is even more distracting than the demanding press of her mouth. "I'm hardly going to talk you into leaving this library by playing fair."

Nyla laughs, helpless and more delighted than she ever intends to admit. It's such a ludicrous falsehood. Yes, Nyla is overly studious and strict with herself. Yes, she is anxious as hell about two of her upcoming final exams, and maintaining her GPA through her last semester of college. Yes, she has a track record of working too long, and pushing herself too hard, when left to her own devices.

But Colby is Nyla's most powerful weakness, true and welcome. If Colby had texted to invite her over, Nyla would have said yes in a heartbeat, and they both damn well know it. This isn't about Colby convincing her of anything. This is Colby's mischievous streak, shining through bright and shameless. This is Colby embracing the easiest possible excuse to make out in the library, and Nyla allowing it despite her better judgment.

Probably Nyla should exercise a modicum of good sense here. Just because they're unlikely to be interrupted doesn't mean it's impossible, and even if they're not doing anything truly scandalous—she knows Colby won't push her that far—this is still a wildly inappropriate use of an academic space.

Instead of making responsible choices, Nyla curls a hand at Colby's nape and drags her into another kiss. Her fingers slip through soft strands of hair, and she can feel Colby laughing against her lips. It's not a mocking sound. It's a pleased rumble that Nyla can feel against her chest, around her tongue, in the giddy heat between them. The familiar intimacy makes Nyla suddenly desperate to pack up her things and drag Colby out of this building. It makes her resent the twenty-minute walk it will take to reach some goddamn privacy.

Nyla kisses Colby anyway, setting her impatience aside. She lingers in the soft exploration of lips and tongue, the trace of fingertips at the hollow of her throat, the thoughtless caresses ruffling her hair.

When they finally part again, Colby is wearing a different sort of smile. Softer. Quieter. It's the intimate and slightly disbelieving smile she saves for Nyla alone—the one that says she still can't entirely believe her good fortune, that Nyla is hers—that she actually gets to do this.

Nyla knows the feeling. There are days she can't fathom her own luck, to have Colby in her life, stubborn and sure and gorgeous.

"Get off of me," Nyla says gruffly, tracing the pad of her thumb across Colby's kiss-plump lower lip. "Let's go home."

Discordant Details

There is something soothing about the
cheerful dance of firelight in an old-fashioned
brick hearth. Tonight especially, the warmth
coils soft and welcome around Daichi, chasing
off the chill that's been clinging to him all day.
He doesn't enjoy winter, with its icy roads and
biting winds, its brutal temperatures making his
car reluctant to start, its snow and sleet burying
every vehicle parked along the curb outside,
including his.

But this is nice. Cozy. Comfortable.
Downright romantic even, as he burrows
contentedly into his husband's arms.

He wouldn't mind winter nearly so much if
they could end every evening exactly like this,
instead of with both of them running around so
busy—with work, with their wide and chaotic
social circle, with their three children—that
Daichi barely knows what day of the week it is.

Kyle is the genius with a calendar, the one who keeps everyone on track with his compulsive attention to detail. That he's allowed himself to unwind enough to sit here on the living room floor and cuddle feels like a miracle.

Daichi rests his head on Kyle's broad chest, pressing his ear over Kyle's heart, so he can listen for the steady rhythm.

"You're such a sap," Kyle teases, as though he didn't start the morning by slipping a poem into Daichi's lunch for work. Adorable hypocrite. Daichi sighs contentedly when Kyle's arm curls tighter around his shoulders, squashing him close so that Kyle can press a kiss to the crown of his head.

Daichi offers no retort. Clever rebuttals have never been a talent of his even when he's wide awake. Half-drowsing, he doesn't stand a chance.

Instead, Daichi kisses the hollow of Kyle's throat—right at the gap where Kyle has undone the topmost buttons of his shirt—and stretches his feet toward the fire. Their nest of blankets and pillows slides around a bit with the movement, and he briefly considers that they might have been more comfortable sitting on the couch, rather than leaning up against it.

But Kyle had looked so pleased with his artful pileup of what *probably* isn't every pillow and blanket in the house, though sort of seems like it. And the arrangement looked downright inviting, especially with the fire crackling enthusiastically in the grate.

The floor is perfect, Daichi decides, flexing his toes delightedly in the glowing warmth of the fire.

"Your socks are on inside out," Kyle observes.

Daichi stills, startled not by the information Kyle has just shared, but by his husband's confused tone. "Y…es?" He blinks down at his feet, where it should surely come as no surprise to see the messy interior of the stitched pattern showing, loose strings and all. They aren't especially nice socks. Probably a pair snatched up at a museum gift shop or something. The insides look like a tangled riot of string and color.

"On purpose?" Kyle asks, and amusement lights up Daichi's chest as he realizes he can practically hear Kyle furrowing his brow.

"I don't like the way the seam feels on my toes." He pauses, absorbing the implication of Kyle's question. Then, drawing back so he can meet Kyle's gorgeous—if momentarily perplexed—brown eyes, Daichi says with unconcealed incredulity, "We've been married sixteen years. Have you really never noticed before?"

Daichi always wears his socks inside out. Literally every day. Granted, it's not always as obvious as it is with this gimmicky pair, but the point stands, and it threatens to bring a fresh rush of humor bubbling up in his chest.

"Are you being serious right now, or are you trolling me?" Kyle eyes him dubiously. "I feel like you're trolling me."

"Oh my fucking god, babe." Daichi's laughter finally jars loose, shaking him with mirth. He's glad they have the house to themselves tonight, so he doesn't need to mind his language. "I'm not trolling you. You've seriously *never noticed* that I always wear my socks inside out?" It seems very much like the kind of discordant detail tailor-made to drive Kyle's precise and organized personality up the wall. Hell, maybe that's why he's never noticed.

Maybe this particular oblivion is a defense mechanism.

Either way, Daichi doubts he'll ever stop giving Kyle shit about this. The terrain for potential teasing is too fertile.

When he looks into Kyle's face, he finds a scowl there, but it's an exaggerated and put-upon sort of expression, and Daichi knows him far too well to be fooled. The glower is struggling to suppress laughter—a glare that can do nothing to conceal the brighter glint of humor, affection, pleasure in Kyle's expressive eyes—and the sight of it strips away the last of Daichi's own tenuous control. His laughter escapes in a helpless, shaking rumble, and he curls against Kyle's chest as he struggles to catch his breath.

It takes only a handful of heartbeats before Kyle is laughing too. And by the time they quiet, Daichi's eyes are watering so hard that there are tear tracks down his cheeks.

He startles when Kyle kisses him, but melts almost instantly. His head is still swimming with a giddy tangle of exasperation and delight, and he buries both hands in Kyle's hair, sliding his fingers through the soft strands. He tugs a little too hard trying to pull his husband closer, and they topple over amid the pillows and blankets, landing with a thump, cracking themselves up all over again.

"You're such a disaster," Daichi says, kissing Kyle's cheek and grinning ear to ear.

Kyle huffs, a familiar sound that ignites bright affection in Daichi's chest. "At least I know how to wear my socks."

About the Author

Yolande Kleinn may be a shameless dreamer and a stubborn optimist, but she is also a proud purveyor of romance and erotica. Excitable, fastidious and a little eclectic, she spends every spare moment writing the stories she wants to read. If she can drag other people into the pool along with her, then so much the better.

You can find Yolande via her website:
yolandekleinn.com

Other Titles by Yolande

HEARTS RIGHT HERE

From road trips to isolated cabins, business partners to longtime besties, old crushes to new revelations, former bosses to dad's best friend... Delve into nine contemporary romances where friendship changes course.

Collection includes:
Something Softer—Wishful Thinking—Very Close and All at Once—Just About Perfect—Running Hot—Anticipation—Matters of Heart—Right Here with Me—Put It in Writing

AN INTIMATE CHARADE

Cargo ship captain Galin Odona is in desperate need of a contract. When a lucrative opportunity comes his way, he invites Addison Valdez—smart, stubborn, and the only Human member of his crew—to join the negotiation.

Anatoria Baell's contract is not precisely legal, and she has unconventional methods for choosing where to put her trust. Galin agrees to pose as a distant relation during a gathering at her private estate. The negotiation takes a complicated turn when Addison proclaims that Galin is not only his captain, but his mate. The hot-headed lie puts them in a tough spot, maintaining their charade for the duration.

But Galin is a terrible liar. Even worse, he's been in love with Addison for years. Now, through tight quarters and an illusion of intimacy, he must win the contract without giving himself away. The task seems monumental, but Galin cannot afford to fail.

OPEN SKIES

After seven years working as partners, Kai and Ilsa are the best professional finders in the business. There's nothing they can't track down, no matter how unfamiliar the star system or hazardous the path. When a new client insists on accompanying the search for his daughter, Ilsa and Kai reluctantly agree. How can they refuse when Eleazar Dantes is desperate enough to pay double their usual fee?

But a high-stakes investigation is no time for distractions. Even more troublesome, when Kai realizes his true feelings for Ilsa, his timing couldn't be worse. Never mind that she doesn't seem to reciprocate: heartbreak is the least of their problems as the trail they're following grows dangerous.

With every step forward, Kai and Ilsa are more certain they won't find Eleazar's missing daughter alive.

ALL THE WAY HOME I'LL BE WARM

Driving home for the holidays, Jamie Phipps can't believe his car has broken down only four hours from the finish line. At least he finds distraction in the arms of a gorgeous older man. When they part ways, Jamie hopes a string of sweet text messages means they'll stay in touch.

For now, it's nearly Christmas, and Jamie has other worries. Like hitching a ride with his sister for the final leg of the journey. Like his car, stranded at the repair shop for want of parts. Like meeting his father's closest friend, Victor Leone, a stranger Jamie doesn't remember at all.

But when Jamie crosses his parents' threshold, Victor is no stranger. And even worse than the mutual shock of realizing he slept with his dad's best friend: Jamie can't stop craving an encore. It doesn't matter how powerfully the attraction simmers between them. If anyone learns the truth, their secret will ruin more than just Christmas.

Jamie knows Victor is off limits. If only he could make his stubborn heart believe it.

ASHES ON A DISTANT WIND

Before the Vrete came to Earth, Donovan Riggs was a man of faith. Now they're gone, and he's left that part of himself behind for good. In the ruinous aftermath of a war nobody won, he is simply trying to survive. With Beau Greer—a young medic who stumbled into his life and then refused to leave—Riggs travels dangerous roads between long-dead cities. Scavenging doesn't offer much of a future. It barely provides for the present. But Riggs will do anything to protect what's his.

EVERY SECOND YOU'RE ALIVE

Major Franklin Cade has spent years fighting the undead scourge that drove humanity from Earth. Now victory is in sight, but it's come at immeasurable cost. He has sacrificed everything in the line of duty—even his own heart.

For six months Lieutenant Daniel Mendoza has been missing in action. Only stubbornness and a refusal to tarnish Mendoza's memory have kept Franklin alive since losing the man he wouldn't admit he loved.

When a perilous rescue needs volunteers, he returns to the canyon where Mendoza fell. He is not prepared for the hope that ignites as he follows a fading distress signal across infested terrain. In the shadow of a deadly countdown every second is precious, but Franklin refuses to lose Mendoza again.

SIMPLE AFTER ALL

Noah Fiore, contracts attorney and dedicated curmudgeon, spends every Christmas with his family on the shore of Lake Superior. It's practically tradition for his sister to invite some lonely acquaintance along for the festivities.

But this year's guest is no pity case. Riley Coto is a friend, whose warmth and charm instantly win over the collective hearts of the Fiore family—all except Noah, who remains as dour and unapproachable as ever.

Riley finds himself inexplicably drawn to Noah. Something tells him there's more to the man than stubborn work ethic and bad attitude. With Christmas fast approaching, Riley is falling for Noah, and there's nothing simple about that.